Robert Wicks is a master craftsman of hope. He exquisitely hones this indispensable quality in *Conversations with a Guardian Angel*. Wicks's perspective remains positive even amid the greatest darkness and loss. The author has a remarkable ability to draw meaning from the events of ordinary life and offer theological, spiritual and psychological insights with both depth and clarity. As with his other publications, this one is spiced with good humor, delightful stories, and practical insights. Prepare yourself for a spiritually enriching and hope-filled experience as you enter into these beloved conversations.

—Joyce Rupp, award-winning author of numerous books, including *Fragments of Your Ancient Name*

There are certain books that require what St. John of the Cross describes as "a deep and delicate listening." *Conversations with a Guardian Angel* is such a book. Reading it is like eavesdropping on intimate conversations between a person and God. The reader feels that he or she is standing in a doorway that connects two worlds, the psychological and the spiritual, the temporal and the eternal. It is a book that invites the reader to listen to the quiet wisdom of God below the clamor of the ego. *Conversations* enkindles within us, a desire for the serenity of coming home to our true self, the innocent, unpretentious child made in God's image and likeness.

—Marc Foley, O.C.D., author, *The Ascent of Mount Carmel: St. John of the Cross, Reflections*

Wicks, with his lucid and captivating prose, tells a story that will comfort and reassure his readers of the presence of God in their lives. His first work of fiction places him among the most brilliant storytellers of our era in the genre of spiritual literature. For anyone who has ever lost a loved one or suffered a numbing tragedy (i.e. everyone), *Conversations with a Guardian Angel* is a balm for the soul and a light for the dark.

—Therese Borchard, author, *Beyond Blue: Surviving Depression & Anxiety and Making the Most of Bad Genes*

CONVERSATIONS WITH A GUARDIAN ANGEL

~ A Novel ~

ROBERT J. WICKS

Franciscan
MEDIA
Cincinnati, Ohio

Scripture passages have been taken from *New Revised Standard Version Bible,* copyright ©1989 by the Division of Christian Education of the National Council of the Churches of Christ in the U.S.A., and used by permission. All rights reserved.

Cover and book design by Mark Sullivan
Cover image © Markus Giolas

LIBRARY OF CONGRESS CATALOGING-IN-PUBLICATION DATA
Wicks, Robert J.
Conversations with a guardian angel : a novel / Robert J. Wicks.
pages cm
ISBN 978-1-61636-868-5 (alk. paper)
1. Psychiatrists—Fiction. 2. Psychic trauma—Fiction. 3. Guardian angels—Fiction. I. Title.
PS3623.I295C77 2015
813'.6—dc23
2015019311

Copyright ©2015, Robert J. Wicks. All rights reserved.
Published by Franciscan Media
28 W. Liberty St.
Cincinnati, OH 45202
www.FranciscanMedia.org

Printed in the United States of America.
Printed on acid-free paper.
15 16 17 18 19   5 4 3 2 1

For my granddaughters,
Kaitlyn and Emily Kulick.
May they continue to listen to
the whispers of their own
Guardian Angels.

For he will command his angels concerning you
to guard you in all your ways.
—Psalm 91:11

THE
BEGINNING

Welcoming Gentle Spiritual Wisdom

In my work as a psychiatrist, I have always had two fairly simple goals: to enable people to enjoy their lives a little more and to help them better appreciate the amazing breakthroughs possible when they can stand in the darkness with a new sense of openness. When this happens, they will benefit and be in a position to be a beacon of hope for others. You can even see it in their smiles, in their authentic appreciation of the short time they have left on this earth, and in their ability to reach out to their family, friends, and those they meet without being pulled down in the process.

When I have been able to help others realize that rejection, failure, misfortune, and even trauma and serious misfortune, were not the last word, life became something new, dear, and precious to them in so many new ways. The sadness for the loss or negative events they encountered didn't disappear of course— and those events certainly weren't seen as anything desirable.

However, these breakthroughs in therapy and mentoring are a recognition that with openness and gentleness we may experience growth, depth, and an ability to be compassionate in ways that could not have been possible had the terrible events not happened in the first place.

It is not *if* terrible things will confront us, but *when*. Thus, our perspective can destroy or grow us. True sadness can become *spiritual* sadness so that we can embrace amazing new experiences and wisdom *if* we are open enough—especially when something happens that seems totally unbelievable at the time. I can personally attest to this in my own life, to why this has made all the difference for me, and to why I am sharing the results of an amazing encounter I have had in the hopes you can learn from it as well.

Even psychiatrists don't truly get it until something traumatic personally affects them and they are able to feel and embrace deeply what has happened to them. Moreover, unless they are open enough to let go of their own views in order to welcome remarkable new opportunities—particularly when they seem initially surreal—they will never be able to move deeper in their relationship with God.

The best way I can explain this to you is to share some of the following notes from my journal. But before I do this, I need to let you know a bit about my little sister, Sheila, so you can better understand why I would reveal personal reflections that, if they should get out, might well destroy my reputation as a quite level-headed psychiatrist.

* * *

Being with Sheila was always great fun. You couldn't help but smile in her presence. We were five years apart and looked so completely different from each other. I was tall and lanky with auburn hair. She was petite and blond. The expression on my face—and maybe this was an early sign that I should be a therapist—was usually nondescript. Hers was always brimming with whatever feeling she was having at the time. She was totally irrepressible. From the time she was a small child, you could never predict what she would do next.

For example, one night when she was only three years old, I was staying overnight at a friend's house. My dad, who was a true country physician, was out making house calls, and my mom, a teacher, was at home with my sister. Mom worked long hours during those days. She not only taught at the local Catholic school but also would visit and informally consult with parents who were home-schooling their children.

In some cases, my mom would just need to provide a bit of information on how to teach a particular subject. In other cases, she had to try to diplomatically let the parents know that they really weren't equipped to continue along this road. In such cases, she took it to heart when the parents resisted her efforts to get their children into a more structured setting because it would be more beneficial for them. Instead of seeing that she was only interested in everyone's best welfare, the parents in question often felt she was personally attacking them. They also felt that my mom was undermining their desire to provide a good religious foundation for their children. My dad, as a physician, had many resistant patients. And so he was used to being confronted by anger, denial, and even personal attacks. He would tell her to just shrug it off, but my mom was too sensitive to ever do that.

At times like these, which she would term "days when hail and locusts fell on my head," she would always look forward to the evening when all of us were in bed—especially my turbo-charged little sister—so she could take a bath, put on some classical music, and read a little nourishing spirituality. Her favorites at the time were Joyce Rupp, Henri Nouwen, and inspirational biographies—which she would read and reread.

On this particular night, since both my father and I were out, she "only" had to get my sister, Sheila, to bed. When she finally did, her ritual was to wait a while to ensure Sheila was fast asleep. This time mom followed that routine but didn't go in to verify that Sheila was finally asleep because it was so quiet for an hour, which almost never happened if Sheila was still awake.

And so, Mom, as I overheard her telling my father the story the next morning, ran a bath but this time put in some special bubble bath she had been saving for a notable occasion (it obviously had been a very bad "hail and locust" day). She then turned on the small portable radio she had and put it on the sink in order to listen to the classical music station that she faithfully supported during their fund drive. She then placed a new spirituality book alongside the bathtub.

She said she had just gotten into the tub, sat down, leaned

back, and sighed deeply with satisfaction, when the door suddenly burst open and my sister marched in stark naked, while loudly exclaiming as she quickly stepped into the tub, "I just love bubble baths!" In the telling of the story the next morning, my mom had to smile at it all, and my father roared in laughter as well. How could you not? Sheila's precocious nature had that impact on everyone.

Even my dad was not immune from my sister's antics. As a matter of fact, I think she particularly liked to pull his chain— especially when he was seeking to appear wise in his efforts to guide her. For instance, when she was five, all of us except Mom were outside in the back of the house. I noticed as I sat at the table in the yard playing chess with my dad that Sheila seemed to be having an argument with the boy next door, so I mentioned it to him. In response, he said to me: "Well, go over and ask her to come here so we can see what is going on." To which I immediately turned toward her and shouted, "Sheila! Come over here! Dad wants to talk to you!" My dad looked at me, made a sour face, and said, "*I* could have done that without your help."

Eventually, when she did run over, my dad asked her: "What seems to be the problem, Sheila?" She responded, "He doesn't want to play with me," pointing to the little boy next door, who was by now making a face at us.

My father then put down the book he was reading, formed the famous sage expression on his face that both of us were now familiar with, and said in a low, measured voice while nodding up and down: "Well, what do you do when your friend doesn't want to play with you?"

After a moment of seemingly reflecting on this question, Sheila, while also now nodding up and down, said in an equally low voice like my dad, "I hit him over the head with a rake."

My startled father said, "What?!" To which she responded while looking at him with an almost disgusted look, "Well I *didn't* do it."

As an adult, she became taller but always remained the same imp. Despite becoming very wise herself, as well as a great parent, devoted wife, and an excellent nurse, she never lost her appreciation for what was important but used her hilarious perspective on things to clearly make her point. People just loved to be around her because of the way she saw life. To hear her commentary on daily events was always a joy.

A good example of this was the attitude she had about her total inability to cook. Her husband, Bill, jumped in most of the time, but she just never gave up trying—and in a big way! She would come up with new recipes that would make her four children roll their eyes. Also, when preparing meals she would set off the smoke alarm so often that she once told me that she worried about her children's safety. When I asked her why, she said, "Jack, when they hear the alarm, they don't see it as a warning. Instead, as soon as it goes off, they immediately come down, sit at the kitchen table, and put their napkins on their laps because they think it is a signal that dinner is almost ready!"

Even in discussions about important family decisions, her

humor and quips broke through to lighten the scene so it didn't develop into a full-scale argument. I loved hearing about these events during my visits. I tried to get to see Sheila and her family at least once a week. On one of those drop-ins, her husband, Bill, was out barbecuing in the yard, and the four children— which included twin boys, who were both five at the time, and two older sisters—were upstairs playing video games.

After making a latte for me on the new gadget I had bought her for her last birthday, she whispered to me, "Last night Bill said he'd like to have four more children. Four more!"

"What did you say to him?" I asked.

She responded, "I told him I didn't know whom he was going to have those children with, but I promised I would treat them as my own."

I have tried to give you just a little sense of what Sheila was like because of what I am going to share with you next. Sheila's irrepressible personality and how much she meant to me are the impetus for why I started recording my thoughts, feelings, and actions at the end of each day. Also, despite what my psychiatric colleagues might think if you should slip and they get wind of with whom I claim to have had those conversations, I am now letting you read selections of these conversations from the journal I have kept for over twenty years. Maybe I am being too cautious or dramatic in putting it that way, but to be honest, that is my real fear as I get ready to share them with you.

Also, I recognize that you may also have experienced what I have or maybe undergone even more pronounced moments than what I am about to reveal. However, I needed to share these excerpts from my journal now whether you have or not. If you haven't, my hope is that some of the wisdom I have received can rub off on you in some way. On the other hand, if you have had conversations similar to mine, I am taking the chance in sharing with you this personal material because I want you to know that I am with you.

But I am getting ahead of myself. First, a bit more about my sister. Now that you know something about her, I am ready to share my most important story involving me, my family, and Sheila.

When I was in my late thirties, as is typical of a physician who has recently completed his psychiatric residency, I was spending long hours at the hospital, a clinic, our local medical school, and a group private practice. The hours were not anything particularly daunting because of the work ethic set by my parents, especially my dad. He would not only see patients in his office, but would also make house calls and even do rounds at the hospital—since it was the time before certain physicians (termed "hospitalists") covered hospital care, thus allowing family practice physicians to only be on duty from 9 to 5 and periodically on call in the evening.

On one of these more particularly trying days for me, Suzie, the nurse in charge of our acute psychiatric inpatient unit, tracked me down as I was walking to intensive care to do a consult. Her doing this was generally unheard of given her usually stoic personality and the great demands of the ward. When I saw the expression on her face, I could tell it was quite important, so I quickly asked, "What's the matter?" My first thought was that one of my patients had begun to behave badly. Some in the past during a psychotic episode had broken some furniture and threatened the staff. Worse yet, I worried that one of them had attempted or committed suicide.

As it turned out, it had nothing to do with my patients. Instead, she said in a very calm voice: "Your dad, Dr. Lynch, called. He wants to speak with you *immediately*."

On hearing this, I reached for my cell phone. However, she gently put a restraining hand on my arm and said, "He didn't call from his office. He is downstairs in the lobby now and asked if you might come down for a moment."

I didn't ask Suzie anything more. I recognized that she would not tell me anything more; she wanted me to act *now*. So, I quickly thanked her for coming to pass on the message and took to the stairs to run down to the lobby.

There, I found my dad sitting quietly in one of the visitors' areas. When he saw me he stood up, smiled encouragingly, and before I could ask anything, said, "Son, let's go over there," pointing to a quiet corner area that was empty. His use of "son," rather than my name "Jack," made my stomach drop since he only called me that when it was a very serious situation, like when Mom was diagnosed with breast cancer.

We sat down. He ran his right hand through his bushy gray hair and said in a low voice, "As a psychiatrist, you know better than I do that when people are in tough spots, they react very foolishly at times and are often sad and filled with regret afterward—especially when it dawns on them that they can't undo what they have foolishly done."

When he said this to me, initially I thought he was talking about himself. I should have known better. He wouldn't have come all the way down to the hospital to share something like that. Now, as I look back, remembering thinking, after seeing his face and hearing the deep sadness in his voice, that my dad was confessing something about himself, I realize it was a last ditch effort on my part at denial. I didn't want to hear what he really was there to tell me.

He went on: "A man in his mid-fifties was laid off from his job. He was so distraught that he went to the bar and drank too much. Much too much. And then finally he foolishly got into his car and tried to drive home. At least, I guess that is where he was going."

"What does this have to do with us, Dad?" I asked in an irritated voice. I didn't realize it at the time, but my father could hardly come to grips with what he was about to say himself. This was his way of doing it while preparing me for the worst.

In response, Dad immediately went on, "The man went through a light and hit Sheila's car broadside."

"Was she in it? Was she hurt?"

Finally, he let the rest out in a fast stream: "She and the twins were inside. No one survived."

"They were killed? All three are *dead*?"

He replied in a voice devoid of emotion, "Yes, son. They're gone."

The silence that followed this statement haunted and trailed me through the days that followed, including the wake, the funeral, and the burial. For that matter, those words echoed in my soul for the next several months. I could not conceive that I would *permanently* be without Sheila and the twins, in this world at least.

Looking back, I can vividly recall entering the funeral parlor and seeing my petite little sister laid out in the coffin with one of the twins under each arm.

After about six months, I picked up what was left of my life again and started to do things that brought me joy. When I was finally able to resume living, I no longer felt guilty or strange if I laughed or was happy. It took a lot of introspection, conversations with God, and forgiveness. Mental health professionals used to believe that grieving required a much shorter period of time to reconcile and accept what has happened. But now we know better. Now *I* know better.

Then, sometime about a year after it happened, something occurred that I still, to this day, find quite amazing. I am not sure exactly when it began—and I am glad of that because if it had a sudden beginning I think I would have felt I was going crazy—but I slowly became aware of a new "presence" in my life with whom I was sharing my feelings, intimate thoughts, beliefs, fears, questions, and hopes.

Originally, when it happened, I thought I was simply reflecting in my mind on questions I had in life. Then, at a certain juncture, I realized I was actually speaking out loud with someone other than myself: someone I couldn't physically see but knew was tangibly present. It was at that point, when I happened to also be alone at home, that I dared to intentionally ask a question out loud for the first time, as if someone else were truly present, in some way, somehow.

"Who are you?"

I must have asked the question a bit brusquely because in a feminine voice the response was, "Don't be alarmed. It's just me, your Guardian Angel."

"How long have you been there?"

"Oh, for a long, long time."

"How have I missed you all this time then?"

"Oh, you haven't. When you were a little boy, you used to chat with me when you played a game by yourself, you felt hurt by your friends, or didn't know why your parents were doing certain things."

"But I don't remember you."

"That's because my being with you was so natural. Then you got a bit older and forgot me."

"Why am I noticing you again, now?"

"Probably because you need to. And also as you have gotten a bit older still, your life has become simpler. Without the spirit of simplicity, it is very hard for a Guardian Angel to make herself or himself known. People who believe they have all the answers and are full of themselves don't have room for an angel."

"Oh. Well, that makes sense, but why is my Guardian Angel female? And do you have a name?"

"From the beginning it is decided whether a feminine spirit or a masculine one would be better. In your case, it was decided that a feminine one would be more helpful, encouraging, and balancing and would help you gain a bit more clarity when you felt lost. That is why I am here at your side especially when you have questions. And yes, I do have a name. It's Kathleen."

"If you don't mind me asking, why the name 'Kathleen'?"

"Oh, I don't mind you asking. Ask me anything. But, it is more important now that we focus on you, not me."

Well, that was how it all began. Well, not began, but really when I became clearly aware as an adult that I wasn't alone. I had—and I still feel, after all this time, a little uncomfortable or funny in saying it—*a Guardian Angel.*

After that, it was exciting and quite reassuring, I must admit, to know that I did have an angel active in my life. It also was helpful that I could now be more intentional about my questions and, I think, become clearer about my direction in life. It is not that she gave me her answers as much as she walked me through the options I had about the way I felt, thought, and behaved in different situations. Somehow I also felt more intimately the reality that I was becoming part of something larger at a time when I still felt quietly cradled in a deep sadness that seemed just beyond my reach.

In some way, I sensed more deeply that I had a mission that was part of a greater story. I felt that I had a calling from God in a more serious way than ever before. Also, I saw my brief life on this earth as a beginning of something that would go on after I left. And that was another consequence for me: I knew now more than ever before that even though I was still fairly young at the time, my death—at some point in the future—was before me, and that Kathleen could tap me on the shoulder, possibly when I least expected it, and tell me it was time to leave this earth. Surprisingly, rather than this insight scaring or depressing me, I felt freed by it…even *exhilarated*. Not because I want to die. No, now more than ever before, no matter how bad things might eventually get at certain points, I was so grateful for my life. What a blessing it was, and I knew it, enjoyed it, and wanted desperately to share it with others whenever and however I could.

I was and continue to be very happy to be gifted with my precious time here on this earth. But knowing my time would end at some point, possibly abruptly, maybe slowly, made me appreciate each day as an amazing gift. To this day, I feel sorry when other people (or even I, though I know better) forget at times what a gift life is. I no longer want anyone, especially me, to miss all the gifts that we are surrounded by but temporarily may not see.

Kathleen's presence did that for me. That's what made me think that if I shared with you some of our conversations—because I can't remember and didn't write down all of them—possibly you would be able to search for and find the same Spirit within yourself when things temporarily fall apart and life's wonder becomes lost or, more accurately, hidden. Maybe hearing the stories about some of the interactions I have had with my Guardian Angel will make you more aware of your own heavenly guide in some way—particularly in moments of darkness, sadness, or confusion—even though you might not hear him or her at the time.

Anyway, see what happens for you. Also, if you think it would help, without mentioning my name, maybe you might even share some of my conversations with friends who have come to start valuing the simplicity of life but need a little help to enjoy both life and their relationship with God a bit more intimately. For, as I have come to see even more with Kathleen's help, what a wonderful life we have...*every* day of it, if only we attend to it with a little more care.

We are not alone. In both small and large ways, when confronted with questions, anger, or anxiety, in moments of great joy and deep peace, with people we have just met or those who have long held a special place in our lives, there is much to uncover, understand, and reflect upon so that we don't feel the impulse to just react to what is around or in us. Instead, with heavenly guidance we can live each moment of our lives in ways that are truly *spiritually mindful*; then, when things happen—especially negative ones—rather than immediately reacting to them, we can reflect within ourselves and with others in ways that are helpful, not harmful. We can be more compassionate and enthusiastic about everything in ways that Sheila would have done had she continued to live.

I'll be honest. Probably the main reason for my sharing the following simple interactions and reflections I wrote down in my journal is because, in some strange way, I feel I owe it to Sheila. Also, in sharing them with you now—and I know this will definitely seem strange—somehow I believe that I owe it to *you* as well, even though we have never met.

Sometimes it takes great darkness to wake us up so we can see things differently, *beneficially*. I guess I didn't want the darkness I experienced back then and continue to encounter at times to go for naught in my own life...or yours. So mentally walking with you again through the following selections from my journal makes me feel that maybe in some way they will also help you. At least I hope so. And I know in my heart that my little sister, Sheila, were she here now, would feel the same way, too.

SIMPLY FLOWING WITH YOUR LIFE

Following the initial encounter with Kathleen after my sister's death, one of the earliest subsequent interactions with her that I can remember, or at least have recorded in the journal, was one that brought me back to my own childhood. I wanted to know what Kathleen remembered of me and how I was different now, so I asked, "What was I like as a child?"

"Oh, you were such fun. You got so involved and flowed with all of your activities. You had such a joy sharing things with your friends, although I noticed you picked these girls and boys very carefully."

"I was never unhappy?"

"Sure, everyone has unhappy moments, but you didn't let them derail you like you sometimes do now."

"What do you mean?"

"Well, back then, when someone was not nice, you were puzzled or wondered what made them want to be a bully. Now you seem to take it to heart more, get angry, or feel as if you may have made a mistake. You worry a lot more. You didn't back then. You got upset, but it didn't last overnight. You were too excited about all the wonderful things that would show up in the following few moments or the next day of your life."

"What happened?"

"You just started doubting that you were OK. You looked more to others' responses to determine whether you were a good person or not. You stopped being spontaneously yourself and tried to fit in so people would like you more. It's pretty natural. Young people often do that once they start school."

"That's sad."

"Yes, it is, but don't be too sad about it. Now you are bright enough to reflect when you are feeling badly about something. You can examine your thoughts and try to see if they are based on facts or fantasy. For example, thinking 'Everyone must like me. If I make a mistake then that means *I* am a mistake. If one thing goes wrong, then everything is wrong' is obviously not helpful. Instead, you have the choice to expose those deflating thoughts for what they are and to stop berating yourself for having them, stop getting discouraged, and stop blaming others. These are the kinds of things that, as a psychiatrist, you help your patients realize. You teach others to appreciate their best selves and to be gentle with themselves when life doesn't go as planned. You just have to remember to practice your own advice a bit more."

"What should I do to recapture the freedom and boundless joy that I had as a child?"

"Recognize that you are human, not superhuman, and honor your mistakes. Recognize that everyone makes them, learn what you can from them, and then move on."

"That sounds too simple."

"Oh, it is simple, but not easy. People have a hard time being intrigued and excited about looking at their own lives. Often when they do, they harshly judge themselves, which leads to discouragement and the thought, 'What's the use of trying?' This type of self-attack then often spills into how they perceive others and leads to their being judgmental in unhelpful ways."

"This is a lot to think about."

Even though I couldn't see her, I felt her smile when she said, "Don't simply think about it...*pray* about it when things that unsettle you occur."

I asked, "What do you mean by 'pray about it'?"

"Ask God to be with you when you reflect on sad, depressing, or upsetting events...and joyful ones, for that matter."

Then, she shared a phrase from the Bible for me to reflect upon. She said, "Take a walk with the following few words of life that Jesus said in John's Gospel: 'You are my friend,' from John 15:15. See what the words truly mean to you."

I loved how freely she overflowed with God's love and peace. She knew that I needed ideas to ponder and practical things to do that would bring the things that she was teaching me to life. Even in this she was also pushing me to embrace the space that contains the mystery of God, which could not be distilled into a formula.

"Maybe we should talk more about prayer?" I asked then.

I could somehow feel her smile again. In a lighter voice this time, she responded, "Yes, I think it would be good at some point."

"But not now?"

"No, because it would just turn into an intellectual discussion and exercise. In prayer, you don't put your intellect totally on hold, but it plays a lesser role. Your prayer, for the most part, is not simply a verbal exercise or some task to master. When that happens—and it unfortunately does because of what people are often taught by those who mean well—God becomes simply a boss to report to, rather than someone who loves you deeply. For now, simply take a walk and silently repeat the words 'You are my friend' until it becomes 'God is my friend.'" And then, she left the room.

Later that day, I did start the practice she suggested. It was funny because I found saying the words to be both awkward and freeing. I tried it as I walked down Walnut Street in Philadelphia. At first, it seemed too mechanistic to be saying to myself, "You are my friend." I also became distracted by the inner messages, to do lists, and analytical thoughts that were cluttering my mind. Initially I became discouraged that I couldn't focus on a simple phrase for more than a few seconds. But then a thought, maybe an insight, hit me: I'm living my life in a cognitive cocoon, or more simply, I'm up in my head. I'm not experiencing life. I am just thinking or, more often than not, worrying about life. I am not even taking a walk. I am taking "a think" and missing all that is going on around me.

Recognizing this reality probably should have been a downer, but instead it felt freeing. The glass need not be seen as half empty. If I could appreciate what I was doing to prevent myself from truly flowing with my life and with God as an intimate companion, I could respond each time by coming home to the words "God is my friend," and I did. When that happened, it encouraged me to take greater advantage of whatever quiet times or periods of solitude came my way. It also made me recognize how much energy I was wasting on being concerned about the impression I made on people. I was missing so much of life. It was like standing on the edge of the Grand Canyon with blinders on.

I also recognized one other thing: I hadn't given myself the opportunity to take enough time in silence and solitude during my daily routine. Originally, I thought it was because I was too busy. However, what I now know is that I avoided silence because it created a psychological and spiritual vacuum in my mind. As soon as I entered and experienced more than a moment or two of silence, the "preconscious," all those thoughts lying just beyond my daily awareness, rose up and filled in the recently opened mental space. When that happened, there I was facing my lies, games, fears, shames, anger, anxiety, and what I had shunted aside because of my personal embarrassment about certain actions, thoughts, and feelings I had experienced in the past.

However, Kathleen had helped me to embrace these negative thoughts so that I could let them go. Not through avoiding or making excuses for them, or through blaming others and myself, but by giving me a larger, loving partner with whom to experience what I would be tempted to avoid if on my own. She had me walk with God's friendship in my heart so that I could be clear about my crazy thinking and sins in order that I would be better able to learn from, rather than being burdened by, them. This recognition of God's love for me meant something greater. I wasn't conditionally loved for what I did. I was embraced for who I really was...*a friend of God.*

This approach to prayer also led me to discover so many other things as well. I began to appreciate the spiritual beauty of ordinariness and the psychological drain that occurs when I am overly concerned about my own ego or reputation. Feeling deeply that I was a friend of God also encouraged me to see that if I were free to look clearly at my sins, it would also be just as important for me to be more fully aware of my gifts so I didn't wind up overlooking or failing to share them with others as much as I could.

The freedom to be myself would turn out to be something quite spiritual. As I would soon see, Kathleen would also help teach me to value something that the world around me, sometimes even within psychiatric circles, unfortunately often shuns or even belittles: *ordinariness.* In other words, in conversing with Kathleen, I would be in an ideal position to gain a new perspective on life—just like I asked my own patients to seek—to accept myself for what I truly am: a work of art.

As I thought this, a patient I had seen long ago came to mind. She was a woman who always seemed to look at the glass half-empty, even when given a great opportunity to view it otherwise. For instance, she came in one day and told me she was going to visit Dupont—a hospital for children who had severe orthopedic problems. Some had great curvatures in their spines. Others were unable to walk. They all had great challenges. But despite their pain, they had such a great spirit.

I had done a short internship there as part of my medical training and was amazed by the attitude of both the children and the staff. The first time I visited, I had prepared myself to encounter children who were withdrawn, sullen, fearful, depressed, or just plain angry at their fate in life. Instead, as I opened the doors for the first time, I found myself greeted by young people who were doing wheelchair races. They were also hiding the stretchers from the nurses. It was joyful pandemonium. I thought I was there to cheer them up, but I found as I walked the floors that, if I let them, these young patients gave me real cheer.

And so, when I pictured my often-dour friend visiting this hospital, I thought, "Surely this will give her a new perspective on life. If these children can appreciate their lives, she who has so much more going for her—at least physically—will enjoy hers more." She had so many other reasons to be happy, too. My friend was a very talented physician and quite physically attractive as well. She lived in a warmly furnished apartment in an upscale part of the city and had many physical and personal gifts. Yet, often she felt down, misunderstood, and jealous of others.

Most times I or a friend of hers would say something to try to help her see the whole picture so she could enjoy the beauty of life more. In response, she would in some way convey to us that we just didn't get it. Even when something good happened to her, the usual response was that she was sad that the good would pass too quickly or she was afraid that someone would see her happy at the moment and no longer feel sorry for her.

My thinking was that once she encountered the beautiful, accepting, and joyful people—both staff and children—at Dupont, she would feel better about her own life and recognize how truly good she had it. How could she not when submerged in such a positive environment? Instead, she came back and told me how sad it made her seeing all these children suffering so much. It was just too depressing to go visit again given her own state at this time. What a shame for her. Such a missed opportunity.

Now at one level, as a professional psychotherapist, I recognized that negative sentiments can really dominate the way some people look at things. A colleague of mine once said that when we sat with certain people long enough, a child from the past seemed to show up, who while trying to do the right thing, wound up doing the wrong thing instead. Kathleen seemed to be reading my thoughts and said, "It is a bit like Paul the apostle who wanted to do the right thing but wound up doing the very thing he hated."

"Yes," I said. "What about you? As a Guardian Angel, do you get frustrated by people constantly sabotaging themselves and not seeing all the wonderful opportunities around them?"

As I was about to learn about Kathleen, she would answer my question but always by reframing it in a positive way. She spoke out of an attitude of hope that seemed firmly founded in something that I wanted to learn more about.

She finally replied, "I have always been amazed by people who continue to try so hard even though they are not able to see what you can see: that we are surrounded by so much if only we have the eyes to see or, in your language as a psychiatrist, have the right perspective. Aren't they courageous to do this?" She then went on to remind me about someone else who was very different from the person I had been thinking about.

"The person you were just thinking about was a lot different from a past colleague of yours, Amy. Wasn't she a social worker in an addictions center where you also interned?"

"Ah, yes. Amy. What a great person! She had a bout with polio when she was younger, had an older brother who died young because of a freak accident when he was doing a stint with the Army overseas, and had encountered many other challenges. Yet, she always had a good outlook. Her friends who didn't know her background used to tell me that they wished they had a good life like Amy's."

"What did you say to them when they said that?"

"I told them she didn't have an easy life, but she knew how to take life easy."

"As a psychiatrist, how might you explain this...*spiritually*?"

She caught me off guard. I could offer somewhat of an explanation as to why people psychologically are healthy or, on the other hand, make trouble for themselves and never seem to grow up. But spiritually? I had to think about it because I knew that she wouldn't be satisfied with a glib answer or no response at all.

So, after I considered her question for a while, I said, "I think people who are happy, seemingly no matter the circumstances, have a spiritual focus in their lives that helps them see things differently; they have a healthier perspective. They are not silver linings looking for clouds, but persons who have a music playing within them that is more important than any of the lyrics—bad or good events—that occur."

"Hmm." Now Kathleen seemed to be pondering what I had just said. Finally, after a few moments, she asked, "Did you discover that on your own, or did you get a nudge from someone in that direction?"

"Both. First, I remember reading that if we wanted inner peace we could have it—as long as that was all we wanted. The comment struck me as important. Later on in life, I attended Mass at the university chapel. The professor who had written the comment about inner peace turned out to be the Jesuit priest celebrating Mass.

"I visited with him afterward and told him how that line struck me. He smiled and said he was glad that I remembered what he had written and valued it as I did because single-heartedness is truly the pearl of great price. He then added, 'When we are centered in prayer in the morning and then walk through the rest of our day with an interest in what God is both giving to and telling us, then we can enjoy the other jewels of life in their proper places.'

"After a short pause, he continued by saying, 'Single-heartedness helps us not miss all that God offers us and helps us not be tempted to run away from what we must face. Single-heartedness related to our dynamic relationship with God also cultivates a perspective that allows us to see the wonderfully graced elements of our life and appreciate their beauty without being dominated by them. It allows us to face the necessary sadness that everyone must face in a way that allows our souls to be *softened*. This preparation deepens us, as well as gives us the courage to stand with others in ways that allow them to respond as they can, too.'

"At that point, I told Father that I wished he could help some of my patients see this. He only laughed and finally said, 'You are doing a fine job. Keep it up. Just remember to be careful of the tyranny of unrealistic hope. When you make a diagnosis, you will know how much people can take or progress. Don't be too hard on them or work yourself into a frenzy. Walk with them at their pace, sharing the good knowledge you have, and that will be enough. It is faithfulness, Jack, not success. After we do what we can, we all need to remember to leave some work for God to do too.'"

I was surprised that Kathleen's question had brought all of this back to me so clearly. Pacing obviously was part of good therapy, but as I was learning from Kathleen, it was part of the spiritual journey as well.

After a few moments of companionable silence, she said, "We have spoken about a lot this evening, Jack. Thank you for that. Father has also reminded you again of the value of the single-heartedness that comes out of taking several moments in the beginning of and during the day to take a few breaths with God, be grateful for all you have been blessed with, and look at what God is calling you to see, be, enjoy, and face in life right now. To do that, you need to be gentle and open with yourself so you can appreciate, as you have begun to recognize, the beauty of ordinariness because when we try to be someone else or inflate ourselves, life can become pretty difficult."

I tried to push her a bit further, "By ordinariness, you mean what?"

"Let's sit with what we have chatted about for now and leave 'ordinariness' for another day."

Gratefully, we did just that. I had to admit that I didn't truly understand as fully as I'd like the concept that true ordinariness was in fact true holiness. Also, as I was soon to appreciate more fully as well: being your true self, as God created you, was simple, powerful, wonderful...but also not easy.

TRUE ORDINARINESS IS TANGIBLE HOLINESS

When I think of my sister Sheila, my mind also often drifts to recalling Jaime, an old boss of mine who directed the psychiatry department at the hospital. Like my little sister, he was pure joy. He only seemed to have one annoying quirk: He was cheap! All of us teased him about it—*especially* Jackie. She was another psychiatrist who went through residency training with Jaime. Trying to get him to part with funds for even arguably reasonable expenses such as continuing education courses to keep up your license or buying a book or CD on new treatment theories was a major undertaking. As a result, most of us gave up asking, except Jackie, who wouldn't take any nonsense from him.

So I was shocked when seemingly out of the blue he suddenly said, "Jack, soon you will be taking over the department so I've been thinking..." Before he could finish what he was about to say, he could see the wary expression on my face and stopped midsentence. All of us knew that the phrase "so I've been thinking" usually meant more work for the same pay. Given this, he quickly added, "No. No. Nothing official. I just thought that since you are taking over as chair of psychiatry in a couple of months, we could justify taking some money out of the budget to go out to eat together. Sort of a transition celebration."

I was incredulous. "We are actually going out to dinner together, Jaime?" "No, *lunch*, Jack, *lunch*." And, at this, I must admit that even I had to laugh. Jaime was Jaime. What you saw was what you got.

Once after the two of us had a very unproductive meeting with the CEO of the hospital, he gave me a look after the fellow was out of earshot. I looked back at him and said, "What's that look?" He then made another face at me and said, "You know, I think some health care executives would make good martyrs. They are so dry they would burn well." Jaime was Jaime. Totally outrageous, transparent, and ordinary. Never anybody but himself in all situations.

One day, I did half call him on the carpet for his outrageous sense of humor. He became serious and said, "You know, Jack, you are right, but I need the sense of humor so I don't wind up taking myself too seriously—it is a preoccupation in our business if we don't watch out."

"I wish I had a good sense of humor like you, Jaime."

"Yes, well it is a shame that you are such a stick, Jack."

"No, I mean it, Jaime. Isn't there anything I can do about it? I don't want to wind up as so many of the 'shrinks' we know who are so filled with themselves and think that because they are psychiatrists they have the answers to all of the world's problems."

I guess he could see that paradoxically I was serious about the topic of humor because he smiled and said, "You don't want to blow this whole business out of proportion, Jack." He became silent for a bit and then said, "Well, then, I suggest you reflect on *four* elements when you find yourself getting too uptight or reactive about something."

"*One*," he smiled and said, "make sure you have healthy harassers like me in your life. If you don't, you are going to just stay moody and make things important that shouldn't be, which is a total waste of time that you can't afford.

"*Two,* when you get upset, don't accept that what you think is getting your nose out of joint is the real issue. As chair of psychiatry, I get emails of complaint. Some are on the mark and are helpful. Others are from persons dealing with their own issues. When I get them, I immediately pray that locusts would invade their houses, let my anger dissipate, and then look again as clearly as I can at what they have said.

"*Three,* learn to tease yourself more often. If you don't do this, then when something really important comes along, you won't have the psychic energy to deal with it.

"And, *four,* know what you can change and what you can't. Or, in our business, know how tough and slow the going is to change people. They didn't develop their problematic way of viewing the world overnight, and it is not going to change overnight. Also, our patients' and some of our colleagues' psychopathology is greater than our health in the short run. They will win the skirmishes because they have built up defenses, developed excuses, and learned ways to export the blame— including onto lovable, brilliant, handsome psychiatrists like us," he said with a wink, "so they don't have to face their own issues. If we just stay in there, seek to be healthy, and try not to personalize their attacks on us, some of our health will rub off. Lesson completed."

"Thanks, Jaime." I would often think about what he had said in the days to come.

When we did finally go out for lunch, I recalled that Jaime had actually been in ministry before he went for his medical degree and through psychiatric residency. Even now he would occasionally preach at one of the local Methodist churches when the pastor there was on holiday. Given this, I asked Jaime if he would like to say grace before we ate. He smiled, happy that I asked.

We then bowed our heads and instead of his quietly murmuring a few words of thanks, he boomed out a prayer that had everyone else in the restaurant take notice: "Lord, help us to be grateful enough for this food so that we are mindful of those less fortunate than we are. Let us be grateful as well for all who were involved in growing, preparing, and serving it. Finally, let us be grateful to you for being so good to us by allowing this food to be shared in friendship, and we ask you to bless it now to strengthen us so we can move through this day with mercy, compassion, and humility. We ask *all* of this, as always, in the name of Jesus. Amen!"

When I lifted my head a bit to see their reactions, I noticed people staring at our table. Some had actually put their knives and forks down during his prayer. A couple in the corner that looked to me to perhaps be considering having an extramarital affair changed their minds! Then, after he had closed with a resounding "Amen!" he looked up, smiled serenely, and, as if nothing dramatic had happened, calmly said, "Pass the bread, please, Jack."

One day, months after Sheila died, as I was puttering around my office at home, grumbling about some insurance forms I needed to fill in for some of my patients, I sensed Kathleen in the room, so I sat down in my favorite rocker and asked, "What's up?"

In her spritely yet strong voice, she replied, "I think it is time for you to take a trip today. I'll come with you. There is something I'd like you to see."

For the first time in our interactions, her voice came across in a very clear, firm manner. It seems silly now, but I felt a small shudder when I finally asked, "Where?"

"The cemetery," she responded softly.

I had been right. She wanted me to visit the graves of my sister and my two nephews, Tom and Jim. I had been avoiding it since we had buried them. I really did not want to go there. It made it too real for me. My brother-in-law, Bill, and my two surviving nieces, Aileen and Donna, paid a monthly visit after Sunday Mass and then went on to breakfast. He told me he felt it helped them better recognize the reality of her and the boys leaving. It also somehow made them feel closer to them and helped them move on, which was not only important for his sake but that of his two girls. For me, I guess I just didn't want to move on... *yet.* Would I ever?

Kathleen said, "I think the timing for the visit is right. And there is something else I want to show you."

I must have thought that the timing was, in fact, right, too. And I was intrigued by what she wanted to show me. No doubt it was also my growing respect for her wisdom that helped me to comply with her request. But whatever the real reason actually was, after some hesitation, I agreed.

When you drive somewhere with someone, especially when it is as momentous as this was, you usually converse with the person in the car. Perhaps it is soothing to talk, or maybe it is a distraction from what is about to occur. However, unless she thought it was important, Kathleen rarely said anything if I didn't initiate the discussion. Since I didn't feel much like talking, it was total silence for the whole drive. I didn't even turn on the radio.

After my initial encounters with silence while taking prayerful walks, I started to look for other times that could be like that. Avoiding listening to the radio in the car so I could have some quiet time with God was part of these efforts. I also found that I was more discerning in what I chose to watch on television as well. I wanted more silence not to simply be by myself but to quietly be in the presence of God—a place where I was feeling more and more at home. As I rode in the car this time, I also wanted the space to listen even more in case I sensed the presence of God either through Kathleen saying something or within myself since I was anxious about this visit to the cemetery.

When we finally arrived, I parked my ancient green tank of a Jaguar sedan in the practically empty parking lot. Most people came to visit their loved ones in the cemetery over the weekend or early in the morning during the week. This was mid-week and lunchtime. I was relieved that my first visit to Sheila's grave would be a private one.

Although it was quiet on the walk to the grave, I knew Kathleen was with me. I could just feel it.

It took me forever to find the grave because I have such a terrible sense of direction. Before I entered medical school, I was a Marine Corps officer for three years. During that time, they would never let me lead out a platoon for fear we would never find our way back. Finally, there it was. A simple stone with Sheila's name, the dates of her birth and death, and the words:

We loved you so, so much.
Yet, you managed to do the impossible...
You loved us even more than that!

Below these words were Tom and Jim's names as well as their dates of birth and death with the words:

Even though you were very small when you died,
You will always have a large place in our hearts.

My first reaction was to fill up and cry. After that, I realized I had begun to experience anger. Anger at the drunken driver who killed them. Anger at the world for being so empty without them. And anger at Kathleen for bringing me here. But I am a psychiatrist, and the training doesn't leave me so quickly even when I am feeling angry, helpless, and lonely. I was taught that when I experience deep emotion, I should note it but not immediately react. Instead, the aim is to take it as a red flag waving to get my attention and signal a one-word injunction: *reflect*. Emotions lead psychiatrists, therapists, and persons in ministry. Meaning that when they are faced with deep emotion in others and themselves, they need to slow down and reflect within themselves and then with the person in front of them.

In my business it is called "self-regulation." Rather than act out impulsively because of an underlying emotion such as anger, sadness, fear, or guilt, we are expected to look within ourselves and explore the feeling to understand what it is teaching us—not simply about the situation but about ourselves as well. Then, we try to put that understanding at the service of the patient and ourselves. If more of us would pause and consider the underpinnings of strong emotions, there would be less psychological hurt inflicted and physical abuse committed, and there would be more possible regret in the perpetrators later on for what they have done.

Kathleen seemed to read my mind, "Jesus used to do what you are doing all the time. He tried to teach his disciples to do that as well since they were a fairly emotional group and needed to reflect a bit more before charging into situations in the wrong way."

"How did he do it?" I asked.

"When his disciples got upset, he showed them that the cause was not something or somebody outside them but that they were reacting because of what they felt inside themselves. When, as fishermen, they didn't catch what they were fishing for, they became discouraged because they were so interested in success. Because they were quick to blame others rather than seeing everyone—even those who didn't respond positively to their promptings as apostles—as children of God, they became angry and unforgiving in certain other encounters that didn't go their way. And they also got down on themselves because they often blamed, rather than tried to further understand, themselves."

"Well, what did he teach them to do instead?"

"Of course, he taught them many things, too many to go into right now. However, one of the things he wanted them to realize through his teaching was that they must focus on faithfulness rather than success and, of most importance, that *he* would always be with them as a guide as well as a support in their hearts but..." and she let the last word linger.

"But?" I finally asked.

"Jesus told his disciples that they must not try to hold onto him as he was in the flesh. As a matter of fact, they must *let go* so that something greater could happen—that he would come back as the Paraclete, the Spirit, to be with them in so many ways he couldn't be in the flesh. They needed to do this even

though they loved having him with them." She then added very
quietly after a few seconds, "Sometimes we can't have it that
way even if we should want it to be so." She then paused once
again to let what she had just told me sink in a bit further and
see where I might take it.

Finally, I said tentatively, "So, are you saying I must let go of
Sheila and the twins like the disciples let go of Jesus, so I can feel
them in new ways in my heart?"

"More than that," she said, and then was quiet again for a
few seconds.

And then, before I could say something more, she said to me,
"Please take the little pad and pen out of your shirt pocket for a
moment to write something." I always kept the small notebook
there in case I got a call from the hospital or answering service
with a message. Most of my colleagues would use their iPhones
to take notes, but I was old-fashioned and feared I might inadvertently erase the message since I wasn't the sharpest knife in
the drawer when it came to technology.

After I took the little pad and pen out and opened to a new
page, she asked me to write down the following:

> Those whom we love and lose
> are no longer where they were before.
> They are now
> wherever we are.

Her words stopped me cold with their impact. I then asked:
"Are those your words?"

"No," she said. "They are the words of St. John Chrysostom. He was Archbishop of Constantinople and an early church father. Wise fellow."

After another period of silence that Kathleen allowed to remain there, as a field is permitted to lay fallow so that it can recompose itself to produce new riches, I realized I had nothing more to add. I was tired; the whole encounter had drained me more than I could ever have imagined. But as I was getting ready to turn and walk from the grave, I suddenly remembered what she had said to me before we left for the cemetery. "Wasn't there something else you wanted to show me?" I didn't think an angel would use a ruse to get me here, though if she did, it certainly was excusable.

"Yes. There is. By that large mausoleum over there by the fence in the back of the cemetery. Let's walk over. It won't take long."

It only took a couple of minutes to walk there. When we arrived, I saw three fairly large monuments. One was to a general, the other to an old western movie star that I knew from growing up, and the final one was for a woman who served as the president of a large famous university that many people in America associated with ultimate success. She then asked me to read what was written about each of these people and, after a time, asked: "Well, what do you think?"

"Pretty impressive stuff."

"Now, let me show you another smaller gravestone right near where we came in."

When we got near to the main gate in the fence, she said, "Please read what is written on this one."

When I looked at it, I could see from the dates of birth and death that the woman was even a bit younger than my sister when she died. However, what hit home and made me tear up again was the following one-line inscription evidently written by her husband:

Everywhere she went…she brought flowers.

After that, Kathleen didn't say anything else in the cemetery, on the ride home, or even for the rest of that day. I was left on my own to embrace so many lessons: the need to let go when the time was right and the beauty of people who didn't seek fame but were a true presence in the world because they embraced, fully enjoyed, and freely shared the gifts God had given them.

It is only in this past year, though, during one of my times of quiet morning prayer, that one of the most important lessons that was seeded that day came to me—namely, that true ordinariness is tangible holiness. I could feel it in my colleague Jaime, in my sister, Sheila, and in the young woman whom I didn't know who brought the gift of herself, her "flowers," wherever she went. Sheila, Jaime, and this young woman I had never met saw the gifts God had given them, enjoyed these very talents, and shared them freely with others. Could I learn to do the same?

Too often I had thought it brave of myself to look at my sins. Yet, to be like these people, extraordinary and willing to share of themselves, I would need to do more than this. I would also need to fully unearth *the gifts* given me by God as well. This would be important because these very gifts as well as my sins were the heart of my true ordinary self. They were the source of *spiritual* self-esteem.

Grasping this for me was not as easy as I first thought it would be. I realize more and more that unearthing our gifts is not as straightforward a task as it might seem to be for anyone. After my visit to the cemetery, Kathleen encouraged me to go in the direction of honoring my gifts, as a way of being grateful to God for them and so I would know what I had been given to share with others. As a psychiatrist interested in developing my own spiritual life, I should have known this. But in my heart, at the deepest of levels, I must confess, I now know I really didn't.

I also know that the very urge to look at and fathom our gifts so we can stand tall with God and appreciate our spiritual self-esteem is a gift in and of itself...one that we should respond to with a true sense of intrigue and excitement. In this way, we can begin to appreciate that it takes a lifetime to explore who God is calling us to be without getting so caught in the ego-driven concern about how we look to others or what people will think about us. I was a pretty good basketball player when I was in high school, partly because of my height, I guess. However, I wanted to be on the football team because that was where all my friends and those whom I considered to be the stars in the school were focusing their energies. I had been given one gift by God—to play basketball—but because of my wavering self-esteem, I wanted a different gift than God gave me.

A spiritual guide once said to me that when we get too involved in building up our own ego and reputation, it is like coming up to a tree full of singing birds with our ears stuffed with cotton. Now I not only wanted to pull the wads of cotton out, but I also desired to hear the music that both surrounds me and was placed within me by God.

Spiritual self-esteem was no longer simply a concept for me. It was a calling to me to be all that I could be for others. I didn't want who I was and who I could be down the road, with some serious prayer and greater self-awareness, to be put under a bushel basket of worries, failures, embarrassment, shame, guilt, or misguided attempts at understanding myself by solely looking at my sins or defenses. I would need to see myself *totally*—both my gifts and my shortcomings.

Kathleen had helped me grasp this reality at a new level, with increased energy, and also with a deeper sense of hope based on God walking with me as I sought to learn more about life…and myself. It was simply wonderful.

FULLY APPRECIATING SPIRITUAL SELF-ESTEEM

Kathleen's challenge to delve more deeply into appreciating my own gifts came back to me in several ways over the next month or so. One of these remembrances was a story my sister used to read her children. They liked it so much that when I would come over to watch them when she and her husband went out on a date night, they would ask me to read it to them as well. I learned quickly that it was part of the ritual of their settling down and going to bed each night. It is a version of the following story once told by Edwina Gateley, a poet, author, theologian, lay minister, prophetic figure, and single mother:

> Once upon a time there was a country ruled by a king. The country was invaded, and the king was killed, but his children were rescued by servants and hidden away. The smallest child, an infant daughter, was reared by a peasant family. They didn't know she was the king's

daughter. She had become the peasant's daughter and dug potatoes and lived in poverty.

One day an old woman came out of the forest and approached the young woman who was digging potatoes. The old woman asked her: "Do you know who you really are?"

And the young woman responded, "Yes, I'm the peasant's daughter and a potato digger."

The old woman responded: "No, no, you are the daughter of the king."

And the stunned potato digger said: "I'm the daughter of the king?"

"Yes, yes, that's who you really are!" And then the old woman disappeared back into the forest.

After the old woman left, the young woman still dug potatoes, but she dug them differently. It was the way she held her shoulders, and it was the light in her eyes because she now knew who she really was: She was the daughter of the king.

The first time I read this story at bedtime after my sister and the twin boys died, my eyes welled up with tears. Aileen and Donna looked at me puzzled and immediately asked what was wrong. I knew they had already seen enough tears over the past several months, so I quickly responded, "Oh, I was just thinking of a sad movie I saw yesterday."

"Which one?" they both asked eagerly. Now, I thought to

myself, I have really started something but might as well try to finish it. "You know, this is silly, but I can't remember the title."

They looked at each other, laughed, and said almost in unison, "That *is* silly, Uncle Jack." and I smiled back at them. I loved Aileen and Donna very much, and as they sat there smiling at me, I got the feeling they knew this and loved me, too. It was a good feeling. One of the first ones I had felt deeply since Sheila, Tom, and Jim had died.

One of the great things about Aileen and Donna was that they were so different from each other. Their personalities were true bookends. The younger sister, Donna, was very bright, quick-witted, and a real fashionista. Even when she was only six years old, sometimes when Sheila would rush out into the kitchen after quickly dressing for work, little Donna would look her up and down, shake her head from side to side, and say, "Ah, no, Mom." She was often right, too, and Sheila knew it, so she would actually go back in and change a few things so they made a better match.

Aileen, on the other hand, was also intelligent, but what made her stand out was her natural curiosity, kindness, and transparency. She was a true person without guile who would be so honest about everything that you didn't dare ask her opinion unless you really wanted to hear it...*all* of it!

Aileen was even the same way with herself. Once, she made some mistakes during a flute recital that I attended. I thought that all in all she did fairly well and said so. In response she very calmly said, "No, Uncle Jack, I was *awful*." She then added, matter-of-factly, "but with more practice I think I can really do well…or at least, not make as many mistakes," and she laughed.

Just like my sister, Sheila, how could you not like these two girls? I only wish she could have been alive to see them grow up. But, I did recognize a good reality: They did have their dad and me, as well as my mom and dad. All of us tried to spend quality time with them.

That story of the secret princess turned out to be the beginning of a new phase in life for my nieces. My brother-in-law, Bill, told me that prior to that evening reading, they had a hard time eating and showing any joy or happiness. But the night after I read the story, they told their Dad when he got home from a late-night meeting that the story Uncle Jack read them that evening was their mommy's favorite, and now it was their favorite story, too. With these words, Bill said, he felt them acknowledge a move toward the present and future with a new sense that Sheila would always be with them, but in a new way.

I wanted the girls to flourish. For me that meant that they would have what psychiatrists call "possessing a good reputation with themselves." For this to be so, they would need to hold accurate beliefs about their goodness, so they could also face their own negative feelings about themselves without getting totally derailed when they failed or someone didn't like them. Their self-esteem would be crucial in facing all that life would throw at them. I didn't want them to move from guilt or failure at one thing to shame and a feeling that if they did something wrong, they were total failures as persons. Time would tell.

Also, my hope, as someone of faith myself, was that they wouldn't go through life on autopilot, guided by society, their friends, or a fear of rejection and failure. Instead, I wanted them to hear the music of acceptance, concern, and hope and, when appropriate, challenge from me as a key person in their lives.

As these thoughts went through my mind, this time I really did think of a movie I had seen. Both the movie and the central character were titled "Shirley Valentine." There was a poignant scene in the film in which Shirley is sitting by the seaside in Greece. She is in deep reflection on her life and how "little" and "unused" it has been in some respects. At this point, she says something to the effect:

> I've allowed myself to lead a little life while inside me there was so much more…it's gone unused and now it never will be. Why do we get all this life if we never use it? Why do we get all these feelings and dreams and hopes if we don't ever use them. Dreams. They are never in the place you expect them to be.

I didn't want this to happen to my nieces and decided, at that moment, that I would do whatever I could to prevent it from occurring.

As time went on during their early formative years, Kathleen helped me in this regard. She would share with me some biblical quote that I could pass on to them as part of a game I developed called "What Did God Mean?" Two quotes that I can still remember from back then are: "God saw everything that he had made, and indeed, it was very good" (Genesis 1:31), and in the New Testament, "The kingdom of God is among you" (Luke: 17:21).

I knew both of these quotes, of course, from having heard them read over the years in church. But I wouldn't have readily come up with them, so I was grateful to Kathleen for prompting me to recall them at the right time. When the girls were having a hard time living up to their own high expectations of themselves or what they felt we wanted of them, Kathleen also jumped in and whispered a way to help them lean back and appreciate the gifts of life—including, maybe especially, themselves. It really helped.

What she whispered on one occasion was quite succinct but very effective in helping the girls see themselves in a way I think God would want them to view themselves. Kathleen, who was a pure conduit for spiritual life for me and others, said to me, "Ask them why they think God made them? And after they give you all their responses, ask them if they know where Africa is on the map. Since they are studying geography in school now, they will probably respond, 'Of course, Uncle Jack!'" and that was how they did respond.

Then she said, "When children in one of the little villages there were asked by the priest before receiving the sacrament of confirmation why God made them, they said, 'Because God thought we just might like it.'"

The goal was to help them recognize the truth of what I was to later learn was called *Imago Dei*—that we were made in the image and likeness of God. If they knew this and held it deeply in their hearts, the result would be that they would have solid *spiritual* self-esteem. In other words, by recognizing that they were "friends of God" (John 15:15) and made in God's image, the girls would feel more secure, as well as continue to develop a wonderful desire to uncover, enjoy, and share their gifts and talents with others. In approaching life and self-understanding, they would also greet helpful criticism with a sense of intrigue, not dread.

Kathleen would help me again when they became pre-adolescents and they were having a tough time of it because some bullies in their school were teasing them. Once, she came to my aid by sharing with me the following story from Native America that I wrote down word for word in my journal. In sharing it her hopes were for me not only to tell it to the girls, but to get their reactions, so I did. As the story goes,

> The Iroquois tell a fascinating story of a strange and unusual figure they call "the peacemaker." The peacemaker came to a village where the chief was known as "The Man-Who-Kills-and-Eats-People." Now, the chief was in his wigwam where he had cut up his enemies and was cooking them in a massive pot in the center of the wigwam so that he might eat their flesh as a way to absorb their mythical powers.

The Peacemaker climbed to the top of the wigwam and looked down through the smoke-hole, say the Iroquois, and as he peered down through the smoke hole, his face was reflected in the grease on the top of the pot. And the Man-Who-Kills-and-Eats-People looked into the pot, saw his reflection, and thought it to be his own face.

And he said, "Look at that. That is not the face of a man who kills his enemies and eats them. Look at the nobility. Look at the peace in that face. If that is my face, what am I doing carrying on this kind of a life?"

And he seized the pot, dragged it from the fire, brought it outside, and poured it out on the ground. He then called the people and said, "I shall never again take the life of an enemy. I shall never again destroy or consume an enemy, for I have finally discovered my true face. I have found out who I really am."

And then, says the story, the Peacemaker came down from the top of the wigwam and embraced him and called him "Hiawatha."

Aileen and Donna talked about how lucky the man was to find his true face and how horrible he was before he knew it. They spoke about how fortunate he was to have a peacemaker in his life and wondered how the story continued. When I asked them about the need for them to see their own true faces, they paused and said they would have to think about that.

My goal was not to protect them from questioning, doubting, or criticizing their behavior. That's natural, fine, and good *if* it is done in the spirit of further self-discovery. What I did not want to happen was for them to get totally derailed by the process of looking at their shortcomings or sins—what we would call their "growing edges," those areas that still needed some attention.

I didn't want them to waste valuable emotional energy on over-concern or worrying about how they looked to others but instead to be the persons they were truly called to be—no more, no less. I knew the dangers of extreme self-confidence on the one hand or exaggerated self-doubt on the other.

To accomplish this, at times I also used humor, especially when they were feeling "totally terrible" (in their words) about themselves. For instance, once they shared with me—quite tearfully—what losers they were. With a serious look on my face, I said in a low tone, "You should know what a miserable and unattractive person I was when I was young," and then when they gave me a doubtful look, I told them some old jokes. I said to them, "Do you know...when I was born, the doctor took one look at me and spanked my mother."

And before they could say anything, I quickly added, "When I was interested in dating, I sent a letter and photo to the lonely-hearts club. They took one look at the photo and said: 'We're lonely...but not *that* lonely!'"

They really didn't fully understand the jokes at their age, but they could see that I was trying to get them to lighten up and not blow things out of proportion even though they felt badly at the moment. Also, humor is a healing emotional seed, and if you can plant it in people alongside the discouragement they are feeling at the time, it can help.

Sometimes they would say to me, "Uncle Jack, you like us because we are related, so you have to feel that way, but we are not that good."

I always told them, "Girls, I know you have faults, and you shouldn't shy away from looking at them. But you need to also look at your gifts and inner goodness in order to find the real name God has given you."

Aileen said, "But our names are Aileen and Donna. What are you talking about?"

Shamelessly, I then phrased it in a way with the right emphasis to intrigue them further. (Uncles will do anything to help their nieces gain a healthy perspective!) "Yes, but you also have a *secret* name that God has shared only with you."

"Well, he didn't tell us what it was! What is it?"

I replied, "Ah, that's for another visit," and the girls groaned in exasperation at having to wait to find out.

What Is Your Real Name...Now

Occasionally Kathleen would tell me a story about when she was a Guardian Angel for someone else before I was born. One of my favorites was about a very accomplished economist who taught at the University of Pennsylvania. In it, she taught me that all of us have three calls from God.

Kathleen began, "Everyone whom I walked alongside as a Guardian Angel had so many gifts. Caroline, though, was one who had made the most of them in so many ways. As a student, she worked really hard to find an area that she loved. In this case, it was business. After that, without it even being suggested, she focused in on a subspecialty, economics. Finally, she found a sub-subspecialty (which is too technical to be worth mentioning here) upon which she set her sights to be the best in the world.

"She then sought someone to marry who would balance her style and be a loving, respectful husband as well as a good father. After a couple of stumbles on the lane to achieving that, she did meet someone wonderful, and they had four children—two boys and two girls. While building her family, she gained respect and security at the university and published some excellent articles. She worked at church and beyond to ensure her spiritual life would develop as fully as possible."

Kathleen then paused, and I filled the space by stating, "Sounds like a happily-ever-after tale, but there is more, yes?"

"Yes. This young woman was focusing on not putting her talents under a bushel basket, which is exactly what God calls all people to do. However, two roadblocks face the very talented who actualize their gifts. One, they get too involved in building their own reputation, and two, they forget it was not their success that was, in the end, important, but their faithfulness to what God called them to be and do at each stage of life.

"*Spiritual* faithfulness requires a person to address these two challenges. In her case, it didn't mean striving or publishing less but asking herself more clearly how what she was doing was a response to a call, not merely a movement toward promotion at the university and among her peers. It also requires that the person find a word, 'a name' before God that suits her now, given all this success."

"I am not sure what you mean by finding a name, Kathleen."

"Let me use the Hebrew Scriptures, the Old Testament, to give you a sense of what I mean. In the case of a man called Abram, he was successful as was his wife, who was called Sarai. However, at the right moment in his life, he needed to leave that success if he was to respond to God's call to become Abraham, the father of his people. Sarai also needed to become someone different—a woman filled with new potential—if she were to become Sarah, the person God wanted her to be.

"Similarly, Caroline needed to find her new name before God if she were to progress in the spiritual life. Maybe, before, her name or the word that guided her was 'commitment,' 'passion,' or 'involvement'—that was what God was calling her to do and *be* up to a certain point. It was her first calling. However, if she held onto that identity when God called her to the next phase of her spiritual life, her true, total calling that still was in the process of developing would never be reached. In her case, possibly 'generativity' or 'nurturance' and all that this type of word means in terms of how she does everything—and maybe even what takes precedence—might be what God was calling to take root. It was her second calling."

"What does this have to do with me?"

"In most of your life, you have truly responded to the first call of God to be as self-aware as possible so you would know your gifts and temptations. Even today you are seeking to know this even deeper, and that is good.

"The second phase of your life and call from God began shortly after your sister died. You began to be more laid back. You were less of a hard charger and technically focused professional, although you certainly haven't forsaken being aware of new advanced psychiatric knowledge. However, your newfound softness and calmness certainly balanced your desire to perform with a sense of excellence in all you did."

"And the phase I am in now?"

"This is the third and final phase, Jack. It can start at any age. For spiritual writer Thomas Merton, with whom I know you are familiar, it started quite early. For most, it starts in their mid-thirties. I guess you were advanced in the other phases but are catching up a bit on this one, since you are now in your late thirties. It is a very different phase. Whereas the first centers on self-awareness and the second on finding and emphasizing gifts that are not prominent, this phase is transformational. It is when you seek to make the lesser gifts absolutely central to everything you do.

"In the case of Caroline, her first phase or name was 'industrious.' Her second phase or name was 'solicitous'—to be more attentive to others than herself, but her final phase and name were captured in the word 'kindness.'"

"But she was kind before, wasn't she?"

"She did kind things. Now, she was being called to live out of this identity."

"What did she decide?"

"Ah," is all Kathleen said. From the tone in her voice I really couldn't tell how it turned out.

Finally I blurted out, "And *me*?"

"Well, in your case, as I just alluded, you were a helper, a problem-solver, and thankfully for those for whom you worked, a doer. Following this, spurred on by the trauma in your life, you became gentler, and people who were with you felt it. They probably didn't know exactly why they felt freer around you, but they did. Now, this very freedom needs to spiritually explode inside your heart. You need to free fall by centering on gentleness and allowing the doing to be the background music."

"Can people actually do this? I mean, regular people, not saints."

"Well, how about your friend Jamar?"

As soon as she mentioned Jamar's name, I had to smile. What a wonderful old fellow he was. He was our neighbor when we were growing up, and I just loved visiting him even after we moved away. Immediately I thought of a couple of times we were together that still made me laugh. I shared them with Kathleen.

Once, I went in to visit him en route from a fairly intense visit with a group that called me in from time to time as a consultant. When he asked what I had been up to, I told him that because I was a psychiatric resource for the Catholic diocese I was living and working in, I had had a chance to meet the new bishop there, and he was a great fellow.

To this, Jamar responded, "I've only got one question."

"What's that, Jamar?

He then asked, "Can he dance?"

"What?" I responded. Even though I was used to Jamar's outrageous questions, I must admit, once again, he totally caught me off guard.

He then told me that he was speaking figuratively about the need for the new diocesan leader to be a person of the people. Would he reach out and interact with those he served? Would

he have true *joie de vivre*, a real sense of life in him? Could he
dance?

The other memory I shared with Kathleen that day was not
solely with Jamar, although he was standing there. It was with
his wife on a trip to a department store. I knew his wife, Irene,
and she was a person of purpose. When she went out to shop,
she was on a mission. Jamar felt that he was on a mission as
well—to make everyone he met feel recognized, important, and
embraced. I ran into Jamar and his wife on this shopping trip,
and she said to me, "Jack, we came to buy one thing, and we
have been here *forever*. Would you tell Jamar that he doesn't
need to have a personal relationship with everyone here?" That's
just the way Jamar was, especially toward the end of his life.

After I shared those two stories, Kathleen said, "The same can
be said of you now, Jack. You still have a number of productive
years ahead of you as the psychiatrist God wants you to be for
others. However, *how* you are present with others and accomplish this worthy goal is so important—including how you are
present to those you don't work with."

I have reflected on this "third call," this "other name," many
times over the years. I came to realize that I wouldn't find it
if I didn't learn to lean back with God in a very intentional
way each day. Knowing what you need to do is truly important.
Knowing you can't do it alone trumps even that knowledge.

However, in today's world of self-reliance, relying on God
is countercultural. We often let the promises made by politics,
economics, science, and other disciplines trump our trust in

God. Unfortunately for many of us, we don't hear the call again to return to God until we have allowed these forces to lead us to believe it is all in our hands, and then, following these forces, we have failed. It is then that the portal opens up to seeing the essential—that is, the need to take time in silence and solitude during periods of our day and life so that we can see that when we center ourselves in God, who is our identity, freedom to enjoy life without being held captive by what it offers and the ability to be single-hearted in our focus on what matters becomes possible again. Yet, the question still remains as does the freedom in our hands to do or not do it: Will we take the time and open up the space to lean back with God because we recognize it is the only way to truly have a healthy perspective on ourselves and life?

LEANING BACK...WITH GOD

"You look exhausted. Bad day at work?"

Hearing the concern in Kathleen's voice took away some of the sting of what I was experiencing.

"Not especially. I just think that things build up after a while. As I drove home this evening, I realized that I felt particularly drained, tired, *empty*. I had done my usual post-clinical practice reflection, and nothing big came up."

"Post-clinical practice reflection?"

I could tell she was smiling again. Anytime I would use phrases that sounded official, she would get a kick out of it and ask me to explain what I was really saying.

"At the end of the day, I try to do what they call in my business 'a counter-transferential review.'" (After hearing me add this mouthful, she was smiling even more broadly now, I am sure!) "By this I mean that I try to have a very structured reflection about what has happened as well as my reactions to these events during the day so I can learn from them. I review the day's activities so I can have a sense of the 'objective'—what has happened—and I review how I felt during these activities as a way of seeing the 'subjective'—what I felt about these interactions. I then try to uncover my cognitions—my ways of thinking, perceiving, and understanding—so I can better understand how I was viewing the events of the day. I search for hints as to why I felt the way I did. I do this very carefully so I can appreciate how I might have been thinking or perceiving situations and myself in crazy ways, such as thinking I can cure everyone. That's it in a nutshell."

"Great. What did you come up with?"

"That's it. I came up with little. I did uncover some negative thoughts that I had and people's comments I found annoying, but they were really no big deal."

"What were some of these negative thoughts or responses by others?"

"Well, first thing, I received an email that started with 'Before the year ended, I wanted to make sure that I didn't let the opportunity pass to…,' and I expected it to end with 'thank you.' It was from a patient I had worked very hard with and had also seen for a reduced fee. Instead, it ended with her offering numerous comments about how I had let her down, and then it seemed to go on for forever in berating me for my poor work and inattention.

"Following that, I had a complaint from one of my colleagues who I know is a totally self-involved person who should not be a psychiatrist and could use treatment himself, but it still seemed to stick in my craw. Then, there were the usual missed appointments, failure-to-pay fees, ridiculous expectations from the hospital, but as I said, nothing really dramatic."

As I paused at this point, Kathleen then asked, "Well, as you look at the 'nothing-new negatives,' what do you think is going on?"

I responded fairly quickly because I had thought this through before when times weren't good. "Most people think that psychiatrists are crushed by big failures or great stresses. In the past and today, it has occurred to me that feeling drained and used up in a bad way really comes from constantly giving to others, disciplining ourselves to keep our own needs in check, and emptying our own resiliency reservoir until one day—and today felt like the day—we arrive in the evening at a spot where we are totally depleted and can't seem to refill ourselves with the strength we need to continue. We have lost our enthusiasm. It is gone. I actually thought for a moment today: Right, next step, get a job with a pharmaceutical company that requires meeting *no one!*"

Kathleen exhaled slowly and said, "As a psychiatrist, you know that your sense of passion and commitment is not gone, just eclipsed, but it does bring up an opportunity to do something spiritual about it."

"Such as?" Now she really had my attention. It was moments like these that were pure joy for me. I forgot all about feeling in a gray zone. She had piqued my interest. What insight would she share with me? Her response was something I had not expected at all.

"I think it might be a good idea for you to visit a spiritual mentor. Someone whom you could bounce your whole life off of to see what general reaction he might have."

"You said, 'He.' Do you have someone specific in mind?"

"Yes, I do. You are already reading some of his books that I recommended to you a while back when you expressed a wish to deepen your spiritual life."

Immediately I knew whom she was speaking about because I remembered she had mentioned a few of his books and from my reaction knew they were really balm for my soul. "Not, Henri Nouwen? He's too famous. Probably too busy. And, he doesn't even know me."

"Well, you could contact him up at Harvard and ask. What do you have to lose? Also, he is a psychologist as well as a spiritual director. Plus, as you know from reading *The Genesee Diary* by him, his own spiritual mentor at one point was a psychiatrist as well as a Trappist monk. Who knows, you might pique his interest given your profession."

Well, of course I eventually did follow her suggestion after a couple of half-starts on my part. I phoned and left a message for Fr. Nouwen, or Henri, as he later told me he preferred I call him. When he answered, I shamelessly did emphasize anything I could think of that might convince him I would be a worthy candidate to see. Now, looking back on it and having become closer to him since then, I am not sure it was necessary, but I wanted to give it my best shot because I really did want the meeting to come to fruition if it were at all possible.

When we did finally find a date that both of us could make, I flew up and stayed at a hotel with a beautiful view of the Charles River, and surprisingly it wasn't too expensive. I had a truly decadent meal that evening. (I won't tell you how expensive it was, but when I arrived, told them I had a reservation, and was seated at my table, there was a book of matches sitting in the middle of my plate that had my initials embossed on them!) Then, after a fine night's rest, the next morning I walked up to Harvard Square, made a right turn, and headed to Henri Nouwen's apartment house. He had told me to look in his mailbox when I arrived at the building. He would leave it unlocked, and there I would find a key to the downstairs door that would open to the stairway that led up to his second floor apartment. He arranged it this way because he told me over the phone that his downstairs doorbell was not in operation.

After I knocked and his door was opened, he greeted me with a smile and words of welcome. He also introduced me to one of his GAs (graduate assistants) from Harvard Divinity School who was there to collect some work that Henri wished him to do. The graduate assistant also seemed pleasant and glad of my arrival. I am not sure whether that was because of his personality's own openness or whether he had begun to learn the great gift of hospitality from Henri. Whatever was true, their joint greeting meant a lot to a lost soul, which, I must admit, is definitely what I felt I was at the time.

After I came into his apartment and he served some tea to both of us, we sat down in his small kitchen, and I shared a general sense of my background. I also spoke of the work I was doing and how I felt I was slowly sliding down a slope into discouragement even though on the outside I was the same and people kept complimenting me on all that I was accomplishing.

Finally, after I paused, looked down at my hands, and then back up at him with a sense of expectation, as others have looked at me in the past, he finally spoke but said only one word: "availability." After that, silence ensued for a while, and that was fine because in psychotherapy and, as I was to learn, in spiritual mentoring as well some of the most important periods are times when there is space left in the room for people to think, reflect, process...*breathe*. After a while, he did speak, and what he said, while simple, would lead me not only to a greater insight into life but also to a practice that I hold dear to this today. As a matter of fact, it has turned out to be the ritual upon which I base my entire day and life.

Henri said, "Jack, the issue of availability is key to both a rich spiritual and psychological life. People in your line of work and those in spiritual ministry see it as a gift. And, that it is. However, it is also a great problem for most of us. As people and as professional caregivers, we give and give and give, and then there is nothing left. The desert fathers and mothers from the fourth century knew that this was the case in the early church, and now we see that nothing has changed since then."

"So what can we do about it?" I interrupted.

"Well, you know many things from psychology which can help you to keep good boundaries, know how to develop a good program of self-care, and remain aware that the insurmountable problems of those whom you treat can't be cured in a day—even though some of your patients wish it would be so and may become angry or passive-aggressive and undermine their treatment without even knowing it. However, Jesus tells us something greater about availability by pointing us to the balance that underlies the whole spiritual life—all of life, really."

"What is it that he says?"

"It was when he was asked the classic rabbinical question: 'What is the greatest commandment in the world?' Like all other rabbis, he responded by reaching into Torah. And, like other rabbis, he used the technique of putting people at ease, and once they felt comfortable, he pulled the rug out from under them!" Henri said this with such forceful energy that I had to laugh, and he smiled broadly in return.

"He said to the man who asked him this question, 'You must love God with your whole heart and your whole soul,' and you could probably see the man who asked the question nodding his head in assent because Jesus had taken one of the heavy precepts of the Pharisees of the day and held it up high as was expected. After all, what faithful Jew would disagree with holding God up as the One to be first in our lives?

"But then he surprised the man because he didn't stop at that point but reached down and took a lighter precept and held it up on the *same* level as the heavy one, saying, 'And, *and*, you must love your neighbor as yourself.' In doing this, Jack, he was setting out the three essential elements of the spiritual life: presence to God (the most important), presence to others (because only those who have sought and found how to be truly compassionate will be really happy), and presence to self (because one of the greatest gifts you can share with others is a sense of your own peace, and you can't share what you don't have.)"

As I sat there thinking about all of this, he said after a few moments, "But you know *most* of this don't you?" In response, I nodded and said, "Yes, I think I am familiar with a lot of it, or I wouldn't have lasted this long as a psychiatrist. However, what do you feel I am missing?"

In response, he spoke first of his own life, partially I think to break down an unnecessary barrier he might have felt was between us as director and directee. To do this, he said, "When I was in a tough way, I stopped for a visit at an isolated Trappist abbey simply to spend a bit of time alone...I thought. Once there, the brother in charge of greeting guests asked me a bit about myself. After I had shared that I was not only a priest but also a psychologist, his face lit up, and he said, 'We have one of those here, too. Would you like to meet Fr. Eudes?'

"It turned out that the abbey had a monk who had also trained, like you, as a psychiatrist. So, I thought, what do I have to lose? Besides, I was intrigued and, as I said, felt something like what you do now, so I met with him. This morning I don't want to go into all we spoke about because it isn't quite relevant to what you and I are concerned with here. However, one thing that happened when we met is.

"You see he could appreciate after meeting with me for a while that I was a quite sensitive person who also dealt with many, sometimes quite demanding, people. It was a recipe for disaster since I would not change and I did not want to stop being truly available to others. So, he suggested increasing the regularity and time for my meditation. He told me that in mediation, when we spend time not simply by ourselves but alone with God, we are able to allow the issues, conflicts, and concerns lying just below our level of awareness to come to the surface. However, as we sit with a loving God, we can gain some distance from both our emotions and troubling thoughts. This is very important because what we can gain distance from, we can eventually gain our freedom from."

"So, you wouldn't get as upset?"

"No. I am very sensitive. I will often get quite upset, but through meditation, the upset won't last as long, and it will teach me about where I am holding on to my own reputation, desires, and demands rather than freely flowing with a God who loves me unconditionally."

"You're a priest. You know how to meditate. What about me?"

"Well, before you leave, I will give you a copy of an early book of mine. In it you will see that even though I was a priest and spiritual writer a number of years before my encounter with Fr. Eudes, my prayer life was pretty basic. It was good but not like that of, say, someone like Thomas Merton. Do you know of him?" he then asked, and I nodded that I did.

"What do you suggest that I do then?"

"Each day in the morning, get up about twenty minutes earlier. Read a few lines of Scripture or the readings of the day that the church suggests. There are a lot of little books that have the scriptural readings of the day already presented in them, or you could contact the Maryknoll Sisters in New York. Ask them for a little booklet that lists the scriptural readings for each day; they give them out free to those who donate to support them. I know because they send me one each December for the following year.

"Once you have read the Epistle and Gospel readings, put the book aside and simply sit silently for about twenty minutes. Your mind will wander but just let the thoughts run through you like a train. Don't try to suppress, hide, or entertain them. Simply come back in your mind, your heart really, to the themes that struck you from the Epistle and Gospel of the day. Do that each day, and your balance and passion will return more quickly."

He went on, "You see, you have emphasized presence to others in your life. I think you also have, because of your training, emphasized presence to yourself through the natural daily debriefings that we as psychologists and psychiatrists are trained to do. But your problem isn't depression. It is a darkness that informs you that it is the presence to God that needs deepening. You are very fortunate to have noticed it and quite graced that you can now use this sense of "lostness" as a tool to help you be more faithful to time alone with God."

After hearing this, I really had no more to ask or say to Henri. What I needed to do now was to begin the prayerful morning regimen he had suggested. When he first mentioned it, my initial thoughts were the same as they were when Kathleen had recommended that I take a walk with God each day: How would I do it? It sounded too mechanistic or 'religious.' Would it even work? Yet today I share with you that not only did it help me rebalance my life but it did so much more than that—both during the good days and the difficult ones.

With morning prayer, I began to realize that I could center myself with Scripture in the silence so each day could become like a spiritual classroom, or "spiritual pilgrimage." Reading the sacred Scripture of the day also began to help me know Jesus more personally and, surprisingly for me, know my better self more deeply as well. Leaning back with God in the morning did then, and still does, help me lean forward into life more passionately. What a simple, life-changing gift it remains. And to think, it is available to all of us. All we need do is take the time to do it. Yet, the question, as always, remains: Will we? Sometimes it takes the right circle of friends to help it happen and reinforce what we find when we do take the space on a regular basis. One thing prayer unveils for us is that we cannot do it alone. This leads to another question: Who would be best to accompany us on our journey?

FRIENDS FOR THE JOURNEY

One evening I sat down after a late night at work, ate a piece of blueberry pie that my waistline didn't need, had a couple cups of peppermint tea, and reviewed the day. Often it was at this point that Kathleen and I would have a conversation. The day was practically over, and I was relaxed and probably more open than when I was focusing on one of the many tasks I had as a psychiatrist and as an uncle, one of my increasingly favorite roles. More than that, it also seemed a good way to share any thoughts I had with her before a short evening prayer and bedtime.

This evening I found myself reflecting especially about the relationships I had with some of my patients, and even my colleagues, that weren't working as well as I'd like. As was often the case, Kathleen jumped into the middle of my thoughts and turned the subject back to me in a way I couldn't or wouldn't for some reason, by asking, "Who do you feel are your most important relationships in your life at this point, and why do you think that is so?"

Although I was tired from the day's interactions, somehow her questions always energized me. Also, I had spent the entire day focusing on other people, and it was nice to be able to take a moment to center on myself for a change. So I immediately responded, "Well, right off the top of my head, there is my mom, Jaime, Harry—who was an old mentor of mine—and Suresh, a priest originally from India who was a curate—now referred to as an associate pastor or parochial vicar—at a parish I attended when growing up. We still keep in touch."

"Why them?"

As a psychiatrist and knowing Kathleen wouldn't be fobbed off by some general or vague answer, I took a couple of moments to think about what she had asked. When I thought I had at least the beginnings of an answer, I said, "Well, let's start with Mom. My dad is great, but I think of my mom first because she is sensitive, has a real listening spirit, and is a true cheerleader for me."

"A lot like you are for others as well."

"Well, yes, you could say that. I guess I have tried to model myself after her. Without consciously knowing or saying it while I was growing up, I always felt I wanted to be like her in so many ways, and she seemed to understand me better than dad. At least her interactions with me were easier to take. It's not as if she would let me off the hook on things, but the way she corrected me was so much more effective for me. If she asked me why I did something, it didn't come across as an accusation, and if I tried to excuse myself out of whatever I had done, she would just tilt her head and give me an impish smile that seemed to say, 'Come on. Do you really believe that yourself?'"

"You were lucky. What do you do with people who don't have a mom like that?"

"I try to get them to look among their friends for a person who has those traits so they can enjoy that person's, if you will, 'motherly presence.' It doesn't always work because they can't always find a person like that or because their neediness overwhelms the person until she has to pull back."

"Then what do you do?"

"I help them realize that while their needs are understandable, unless they prune them a bit, it will be hard to get them met. And, if they are Christians and are fairly religious, I have learned to give them little cards with quotes from writers who they would probably respect. In the case of patients who aren't religious, I have a slew of quotes on topics by people like Robert Frost, Eleanor Roosevelt, well, just about anyone I admire. I like using bibliotherapy with patients."

"What quote would you use in this case?"

"I might have one of the cards here so I won't try to recall it by heart." I got up, and after some rummaging around in the top drawer of my old cherrywood desk, I found and read it to Kathleen.

No surprise, it was from Nouwen's journal *The Genesee Diary*. I read it out loud.

It is important for me to realize how limited, imperfect, and weak my understanding of love has been.... My idea of love proves to be exclusive: "You only love me truly if you love others less"; possessive: "If you really love me, I want you to pay special attention to me"; and manipulative: "When you love me, you will do extra things for me." Well, this idea of love easily leads to vanity: "You must see something very special in me"; to jealousy: "Why are you now suddenly so interested in someone else and not in me?"; and to anger: "I am going to let you know that you have let me down and rejected me."

Then, after reading this quote out loud, I got back to the topic at hand and said, "It is hard not to have someone in your life like my mom. She is hard to beat as a clear encouraging presence. I try to balance clarity and kindness with my patients. I recognize that if I focus too much on being clear and direct, I run the risk of hurting their feelings. On the other hand, if I am too kind and don't pace the meetings with them fast enough, then there will be no growth. We will be going in circles."

"Tell me about the other three friends you have chosen."

"Well, there is Jaime. He is just so funny, gently gruff, and perceptive that it is hard to take yourself too seriously around him. He harasses, teases, and helps me laugh at myself. I don't think I am saying it in a way that is making the point clearly enough, but he is a very important friend to me."

Kathleen finally interjected, "No. I think I understand. In my role, (she hardly ever referred to herself as a Guardian Angel, possibly because it sounds too impressive, though impressive she certainly was) I have seen people take themselves too seriously and seen how it has turned out badly for them and those around them. It is not just psychologically. A sense of humor softens the soul so people can lean back to avoid inadvertently seeing themselves as the final word or as God."

There was a natural pause after that. I sipped more of my tea that was cold by then but still refreshing. Then, I spoke about the third friend. "In addition to Mom and Jaime, an old mentor of mine, Harry, has always been important to me though I can't take him in large doses."

"Why?"

"Well, he is a truth-teller."

"He sounds like a prophet."

"Yes! That's it. He's a prophet—just like in the Old Testament."

"Most people run away from people like that. What attracts you to him?"

"He wakes me up when I need it most. In class or supervision, I always tell psychiatric residents that there will always be, in both their patients and themselves, blind areas. These could be, as the father of psychoanalysis Sigmund Freud would tell us, areas that we are unaware of—the unconscious. These areas are hidden from us but like invisible puppeteers drive us to believe and behave in certain ways. It is as if we learned how to deal effectively with situations when we were very young—even before we could speak or formulate a sense of understanding of what was going on around us. And now without our knowing it, we categorize the people we meet or situations we encounter according to these early mechanisms, and we behave in the present the same way we did when we were younger, even though the people and our situations have possibly changed radically."

I was warming to the topic so continued further, "Today, another school of thought is called cognitive-behavioral. In that one, the focus is on uncovering ways of thinking, perceiving, understanding, and believing that we are not clearly aware of. Then we can see and test our perspectives to find out if they are really true. For instance, sometimes when I fail with a difficult patient, if I am not careful, I jump to the conclusion that I am a terrible psychotherapist in general. Harry is able to cut through all that when it starts to happen to me, and he tells me quite directly that I am so busy trying to protect my big ego or reputation that I fail to see how crazy the way I am viewing things is."

Kathleen responded, "The prophets of old were trying to get people to turn away from their sins. To stop being hard-hearted. To turn instead to God. What do you think Harry is trying to do for you?"

"I think he wants me to stop thinking negatively or believing untrue things about myself to the extent that I have to blame others for the situation, or pick on myself in an effort to make things better. I think he wants me to embrace my limits in a way that paradoxically allows me to see my real gifts more clearly and appreciate them more fully in order to then see what I can do to improve my therapy, self-awareness, or, in essence, appreciation of my true self."

"Ah, *Imago Dei*."

She stopped me in my tracks. I did take Latin in school but wasn't quite sure what she meant, even though she had used the term before, so I asked her to explain.

"*Imago Dei* is a description in Latin of the fact that as human beings you have been made in the image and likeness of God. Harry seems to be trying to tell you that you are not God, so you can't be right or perfect in all situations. However, according to your description of what he is trying to do, he is also wanting you to claim your talents for what they truly are—*gifts* from God. He wants you to own them so you can see what you have been given to enjoy and share with others, while also seeing that no matter how good you are, no matter the great extent of your gifts, you are not God, so you will make mistakes at times."

"You mean avoid what we call today 'the savior complex' where we think we can heal everything and everyone?"

"Yes. However, in pruning—a word I know you like—the dead branches, such as your unrealistic expectations, unreasonable negative thoughts, and less than kind or accurate beliefs about yourself, you can then allow the healthy branches to flourish even more."

I had to laugh and responded, "You sound like an advocate of 'positive psychology.'"

"Positive psychology?"

Since Kathleen knew so much, when she didn't seem to know what I was referring to, I was often unsure whether she wanted me to explain something as a way of emphasizing it for myself or whether she really didn't know. But it didn't matter to me, so I went on, "Positive psychologists have told us that psychiatrists, psychologists, counselors, social workers, and even those who work in ministry as spiritual directors often see their sessions as merely 'repair shops.' They merely fix problems and send people back into the fray psychologically or spiritually repaired.

"Instead, positive psychology says that we must not only focus on what is wrong in a situation or within a person's style, but also it is just as important for us to see and share what is right about them. The point is that if we see not solely our faults or sins but our gifts as well, we will get a more balanced picture of ourselves. Also, it is by using our gifts more effectively that we can deal most effectively with our own shortcomings."

"Explain a bit more."

I should have known I wouldn't get away with making such a broad statement whether talking to Harry or Kathleen, so I smiled and added, "Often our defenses, personal shortcomings, or what is not working for us comes about when our very gifts—under certain circumstances—become our most persistent problems. So, if I have accomplished some nice tasks, it is OK, even fun, to share these successes with others. However, if I feel insecure, I might share them in a way that turns into bragging because I want to make sure people know I am an accomplished person. Of course, the opposite often happens, and if they didn't think much of me in the first place, they could now add that I monopolized the situation by talking about myself."

I think Kathleen felt I had looked at the situation long enough, because she moved on, probably so our conversation wouldn't turn into an intellectual exercise rather than remaining focused on friendship. What she asked next moved us to the last friend. "What about Suresh, the priest who came to the U.S. and was stationed at your parish while you were growing up?"

My face lit up when I responded to this question because Suresh—Fr. Michael as he was known after his conversion, since Suresh was his Hindu name—always played such a beautiful part in my life. I told her, "He was an *inspiration*—not simply by what he said but also by who he was as a person. Simple gestures made me see his goodness and helped me love the priesthood. Even when I was having a hard time like many other Catholics during the height of the abuse crisis in the church, he helped me avoid getting sidetracked regarding my gratitude for the presence of priests.

"For instance, I wound up treating a number of survivors of sexual abuse by the clergy and was sharing my stories with him while protecting the identity of the patients involved. Do you know what his response was? He started to cry and said, 'Oh, the poor, poor victims. May God fill them with love and...' He paused for a while. 'May God forgive those priests and give them a chance in this world or the next to somehow do a penance that will in some way help those who are suffering because of those priests' sins.' What an amazing man he is."

Kathleen caught me off guard by what she said next. As I look back on it now, I think she wanted me to focus back on myself and the formation of my own deep relationships instead of becoming intellectual about everything, which was one of my temptations during sensitive times.

"Given your honoring of this priest with your respect and admiration, did you ever think about becoming a priest?"

After I had a chance to digest this surprising question, I responded, "I did. Then I became involved with a young woman and realized that maybe that was not where I was being called."

"But you didn't marry her."

"No. She was totally delightful. Filled with good energy. Attractive and fun. My gosh, she was a quick wit."

"How did you meet?"

"She was not originally from this country. She is Serbian and worked in the psychiatric hospital where I was doing part of my residency. I had a Serbian patient who spoke little English. When I told this to the ward nurse, she remembered that one of the unit secretaries was of Serbian descent. We called her in, and she translated for me as I interviewed the patient. It wasn't the best situation, but it helped me get some sense of the needs, challenges, and directions the patient needed to take. After that, the Serbian secretary and I went to lunch, hit it off, and dated for two years."

"What happened?"

"Well, she was great in so many ways, but the relationship just didn't seem to go anywhere. Then, when neither of us knew what to do next, Jaime said to me after I shared my discouragement for the tenth time, 'Jack, the problem is the two of you are in different places: You are not spontaneous and enough fun for her, and she is very deep...*on the surface.* You need more out of a relationship, and she needs something different than a bore like you.'" I laughed as I told the last part because Jaime could always harass me in ways that woke me up and that others couldn't because I knew he truly loved me as a brother.

Finally, after all this discussion, I was tired, and Kathleen could no doubt sense it because she said, "Well, this was great, but it is time for bed for you. I am always happy to share your life with you, Jack. This was even more special. It was good to hear about the cheerleader, the prophet, the teaser or harasser, and the inspirational figures in your life. People need those types of persons within their circle of friends or at least need to recognize that a balance of those voices will make life richer for them since they help a person take less unproductive detours in their spiritual life. You are a lucky fellow."

"Yes, I am, Kathleen. Goodnight."

"Goodnight, Jack."

And as I fell asleep that night, no doubt prompted by our conversation, I smiled at remembering a little sign I saw on a teacher's desk when I was in high school which seemed a good closing prayer for this evening's time with Kathleen:

A friend knows the song in your heart
and can sing it back to you
when you have forgotten how it goes.

Yes, I thought, that certainly is true. And I fell fast asleep.

MENTORS NEAR...AND FROM AFAR

After thinking about the discussion I had with Kathleen on friendship and looking back on my visit with Henri Nouwen as well as the other interactions I was having with Kathleen, one afternoon when I was alone and sensed her presence, I said, "I am lucky I have you. What about those who are not in touch with their Guardian Angel or cannot fly up to Boston to see someone like Henri? Or, even in my case, how can I find others of like spirit who can reinforce, challenge, inspire, tease, and support me on a regular basis or when I need them?"

"That is a true grace-filled question, Jack. The fact that you are even asking it is pure gift."

I was puzzled, and she could see the expression on my face, so she added, "Most people don't realize how important it is to have a circle of friends that encourage us to live in a way that is truly rich and responsive to what God had in mind."

She went on, "One of the easiest, yet most powerful, ways to access good mentorship is through reading. Even today when life is so busy, most people can spare at least ten minutes each night to read, and that is a lot of reading over a year. Certainly better than just reading only when on an occasional vacation.

"The right type of reading can prevent people from living too narrowly or in a self-absorbed way. In the case of all reading, especially sacred Scripture and books about the spiritual life, people can imagine themselves within the stories, take the lessons to heart, and change their lives into a real pilgrimage or spiritual journey like you have now.

"Some people I have guided have also found it important to underline important phrases or themes and copy them out later into a notebook for review and even study what they have highlighted so they can further absorb their value. They can put into practice some idea, theme, or activity that will deepen their sense of God and life and make their compassion toward others more real."

"Anything special I should read?"

"There is so much available. I am sure there are true mentors among the good fiction, nonfiction, biographies or autobiographies, journals, books of inspirational quotes, poetry, and, of course, spiritual works and especially sacred Scripture."

It was obvious to me that she did not want to take away my initiative or dictate what I should read. As when therapists work with patients, it is important not to make them too dependent on you or fail to show trust in the talents they have within them. However, I wanted at least a more concrete idea to get me started, so I pushed her a bit further and requested at least some specific ideas she might have. The result was a response I certainly had not expected. Firstly, because I thought she would mention spiritual writers and, secondly, because I thought those spiritual writers would certainly be Christian ones.

"Well, you might start with some biographies of persons who would inspire you, such as classic books about Dorothy Day and Thomas Merton. Or you might try more recent biographies: *Beyond the Darkness* by Shirley du Boulay about the life of Bede Griffiths, *The Crooked Cucumber* by David Chadwick about Zen Master Shunryu Suzuki, and *Rebbe* by Joseph Telushkin, a biography of Rabbi Menachem Schneerson.

I expected the ones on Catholic activist Dorothy Day, contemplative monk Thomas Merton, and Fr. Bede Griffiths, an English Benedictine, who I later found out had traveled to India to establish a contemplative community there. The others were a surprise, and I said so.

"Why biographies of people such as Shunryu Suzuki and Rabbi Schneerson? They are not Christian."

"No, they are not, but they have lived out values that you would want to both emulate and seek in your own Christian tradition. For instance, the simplicity of the meditation approach of Shunryu Suzuki should have you ask of Christianity: Where is this evident, possibly in an even richer form, in my own tradition? If you did this, you would find the writings of the desert fathers and mothers of the fourth century. You would appreciate how they sought God and God alone and how it freed them to be more available and present to others because of the way they

approached God and life. If you look at the life and teachings
of Menachem Schneerson, one of the most influential rabbis
in contemporary life, you will find a man of wisdom, honesty,
and commitment who emphasized love in such a way that the
number of members of his Chabad-Lubavitcher community
grew—even after his death! As a Christian, certainly you would
want to be like such a rabbi and to search the life of Jesus to
learn how Jesus brought such traits to an even deeper level.

"All good biographies should bring you in touch with your
relationship with Jesus and life even more. Furthermore, sometimes I have observed through the years as a Guardian Angel
that in an effort to become better Christians, people forget
to be better people. They get lost in the rules, principles, and
rituals and forget that God is love and that is the heart of Jesus's
message."

After hearing her pack her response so densely, I needed to
stop for a few moments to be silent. She was well used to that by
now. At least, she never interrupted my needed time for reverie.
Finally, when I was ready to shift to living mentors, I asked,
"What advice would you have in the search for living mentors?"

"There are some basics that you know must be in such
a person. The individual must be able to set aside their own
ego and personal desire—even if it be for good—so they can
be transparent enough that the Spirit can shine through them.
In other words, they must be selfless enough not to tell you
what *they* would like but instead be able to listen to the presence of the Spirit in the room to help you see what God would

want. Yet, although such a person can guide you by offering some sense of the spiritual terrain, in the end, you must take the journey alone."

She then added, "But, let me ask you a question now: What would you like to find in a spiritual mentor?"

Kathleen's question had me pause again. This time I did it while brewing some herbal tea and moving to a softer chair in the living room. Up to this point, we had been in my den where the leather chairs look good but don't allow for a long, leisurely reflection. Finally, I wrote down the following mini-list of what I would hope for in a spiritual mentor, what some refer to in Christian circles as a "spiritual director":

Their attitude toward life in the Spirit should be contagious—in other words, you want to be like them simply as a result of being with them.

Just as in psychiatry, I would want them to offer a gentle, accepting place, which offers you the interpersonal space to share, fail, grow, laugh, and cry.

As we have shared before on the topic of ordinariness, for me they must also demonstrate a sense of simplicity, humility, and transparency.

They need to be practical as well in what they suggest for me to do so I feel it is worth my time seeing them.

And finally, the focus needs to be on my relationship with God—not my relationship with, or appreciation of, the mentor.

"I can't think of anything else at this point. I am sure there are more things to consider, and maybe I am showing that I am expecting too much in what I have already listed, but those are some of the things that strike me now as I sit here with my tea and you."

Now it was her turn to be quiet, and I accepted that. During that space, I was distracted by wondering how I could discern between the times when I felt she was not present and those when she was simply offering some space for the many thoughts to settle. I came up, as usual, with no definitive answer but was still pondering this when Kathleen spoke up again.

"You have made a good beginning with your list. Once you begin seeing a mentor, the list will refine itself. As you encounter what you don't feel is helpful and what you find truly encouraging and appropriately challenging to you, you'll know.

"However, maybe even more important than the guide is the apprentice…*you*. Will you be open as a willing student is when being tutored by a master in the field? Will you, not in psychiatric but in spiritual terms, see the guidance as medicine and have the humility to be a willing patient? And, of even greater importance, will you act in ways that show you are taking the medicine you are being offered?

"In the end, it will be up to you to nourish and continually feed an attitude of acceptance that will lead to such actions—not simply in pieces but eventually as a way of life. Are you willing to do that…*truly* do that?"

Following her serious questions, especially the final one on which she put such great emphasis, once again, it was quiet. I didn't even feel I wanted to answer what she had asked at this point. Not because I thought the questions were rhetorical and didn't need a reply. No, because they ended with such a sense of finality, I felt any comment or question by me at this point would just somehow destroy or degrade the seriousness and importance of what I had just heard.

Time would tell as to whether or how I would answer them. Verbal assent wouldn't do. For faithfulness to any guidance I would receive from a mentor—including her—I would need to act as a way of really responding to her questions. I would need to be willing to respond to what all these questions could be subsumed under: a *call*.

CHAPTER
EIGHT

Seeing the Signs, Hearing the Call

One afternoon during a long weekend at a private retreat at an abbey of male contemplatives, as I was walking along the Shenandoah River in Virginia, Kathleen asked a question that I guess I should have expected. However, I trusted her timing since it always was so on the mark. The question she asked me was, "What do you think might have contributed to your decision to become a psychiatrist?"

If a Guardian Angel could communicate solely through her voice that she was ready to sit down, lean back, put her hands behind her head, and give me all the time in the world to listen to my reply, this was when she was able to do it. In response, I was going to say, "Where should I begin?" but I knew what I would say to my own patients or the residents I mentored if they asked me that: "Simply begin where you would like."

And so, after a few moments of silent reflection as I continued to stroll along the water, I finally gathered my thoughts together enough and said, "Let me begin by saying that even when I was very young I was always interested in helping people. Sometimes it even got me into trouble."

"What do you mean 'got you into trouble'?"

"Once, when I was in the second grade, I was late coming home from school without having gotten word to my mother that I would be. When I finally did walk through the door, you could see the initial look of relief on her face transform into anger. Looking back I realize now that she was afraid that something terrible might have happened to me and felt I was being irresponsible in not calling her.

"Mom immediately asked me, in the toughest tone of voice she could muster, '*Where* were you?'

"I was surprised by the harshness in her voice because she rarely spoke that way, so I became tearful and blurted out, 'I was just helping a friend who was really upset.'

"She was caught a bit off guard, I think, by this response and asked, 'Well, what did you do for her?'

"I looked back at her, still a bit afraid, and said, 'I sat down next to her after class and helped her cry.'

"In response, my mother stared at me seemingly stunned for a moment. Suddenly, her face softened, and her eyes filled up with tears. She then hugged me and said in a hoarse voice, 'I'm really proud of you, Jack.'"

After sharing that story, Kathleen and I sat for a while in silence. I was quiet because it brought me back in touch with a very special experience in my relationship with my mother.

Kathleen was silent too. I guess she could sense this and knew it was important to leave some space for me to be quiet with my memories and emotion. Finally, I was ready to begin again.

"The next three signs God posted for me that I should consider psychiatry came in adolescence and again as a junior in college. When I was in high school, there was one teacher, Mr. Ozuma, whom I really respected. He taught English in a way that truly inspired me, but I also knew him through the social justice club.

"I had joined that club at the urging of my mother. One day I had come home complaining about my studies and teachers. Mom finally had had about enough of my whining and told me what I needed was a larger context so I could get out of focusing only on myself. I was annoyed at her at first, but after I calmed down, I realized she was probably right. Since I liked Mr. Ozuma and knew he was the moderator of the social justice club, I approached him and asked if I could join.

"After hearing my request, he smiled, said, 'Of course you can,' in the English accent that I loved to hear him speak in. He gave me a card that I later found out he handed out to all new members of the club. On it was a quote from physician and humanitarian Dr. Albert Schweitzer that said:

I don't know what your destiny will be,
but one thing I know:
the only ones among you who will be really happy
are those who have sought and found
how to serve.

"The next two signs or calls happened later," I added, anxious to move on in my story. But before I could continue my report, Kathleen stopped me by asking, "Why do you refer to these events as 'signs' or 'calls'?"

"Well," I responded, "I was tipped off to do this by a nun I had as a first grade teacher. One day in class after we had a reading from the New Testament about the Annunciation where Mary was told by an angel that she would be Jesus's mother, one of the little girls up front, who was very bright, raised her hand and waved it impatiently. After Sister acknowledged her, the girl asked, 'Mary had an angel visit her. We also know Joseph had a visit from angels in his dreams. Why don't we have that happen to us anymore?'

"All of the children stared at Sister because it was such a good question, and we really wanted to know what she would say. In response, she smiled broadly. It was obvious that she really enjoyed the question from Missy this time because sometimes Missy could really ask ones that were pretty wild.

"When Sister finally spoke, she said, 'God is still always posting signs along the way for us. In the early days of the Church, people didn't rush around as much as we do today. They also relied back then more on God than on other things or people. If and when you look, you will still see God pointing the way for you in so many different ways. The signs or calls from God are there for those who look for them.

"'For instance, Missy's question today shows she saw a sign or received a call from God which told her to ask a question about what she had heard. Being puzzled was her cue, her sign. In my answering her question, you now have another sign—this time to look for messages from God through me, your parents, your friends, *everywhere.* So, when a feeling, thought, reaction, or question occurs, ask yourself if God is trying to tell you something. It is a good practice of what we call "daily discernment." "Discernment" is a word that means seeking to sift through the messages of each day to find information that will help you be a good person, helpful to others, and pleasing to God.'"

Kathleen then said, "Sister sounds like an amazing woman."

"Yes, she certainly was and is. She had a real impact on me. I still visit her when I can. She lives now in a retirement home an hour or so from where I live."

"Whatever became of that little girl Missy?"

"She became a lawyer. Rarely see her anymore, but I hear she's making quite a name for herself."

I waited to hear any other question Kathleen might have, but it was quiet for a while as if she were thinking about something, maybe Missy, or expected me to do so. Finally, she did speak up and ask, "Well, what about the other two signs?"

"They both came in my junior year abroad. The first semester was in Ireland, and the second one was in Australia. It was a memorable year for so many reasons." At that point, I had to stop for a few moments because some of the experiences I had encountered seemed to flood over me. When I finally was able to step back in my mind far enough from them, I went on.

"The first of the two experiences happened in Ireland shortly after I arrived. Once the initial month of work at Trinity College in Dublin had passed, we had a four-day break. Sean, a classmate of mine, and I took advantage of this to take a train ride across to the west coast to stay in a little cottage in the town of Cora Finne. While there, since we were studying his poetry, we went to see Yeats's Tower, originally known as Ballylee Castle, located in County Galway. We also wanted to see the Burren, located in County Clare, which was a barren area that had flowers from both the arctic and tropical areas growing side by side. However, we got really lost.

"Sean said, 'We really need to get some directions from a local.' I agreed and saw a man standing by the gate in a fence that surrounded his farm, so I pulled up in our rental car to ask directions. Not only did we get sent in the right direction, but the three of us also wound up talking about myriad things. We must have been there for over an hour.

"As we drove away, Sean commented that it was nice of the old gent to take out that much time to chat with us. I agreed but felt something else important had happened that I just couldn't quite put my finger on. Suddenly it dawned on me later that night, and I told Sean what I had been thinking, 'I don't think that man really took out time to speak with us, Sean.' Sean responded, 'What then?' 'I think when he encountered us, he made us a part of his life.'

"Kathleen, after saying that to Sean, I realized later that night before falling asleep that I wanted to be available to people like that in whatever work I wound up doing. And even though I am pretty busy much of the time, I always leave some space in my schedule so I can do just that when people unexpectedly enter my life. As a matter of fact, just before I left Ireland to go on to Australia for the spring semester, I saw and bought a gift card with an Irish proverb on it that captures that spirit for me. It said: *It is in the shelter of each other that the people live.* It is a saying from the Blasket Islands where the weather is pretty tough and the people rely so much on each other for support."

I was starting to tire from relating what were poignant and especially momentous experiences from the past. However, I really wanted to finish the story about my calling, so I continued on about a dramatic encounter for me about halfway through my stay in Australia. Kathleen seemed to sense that I wanted to press on because she didn't interrupt me to say we should probably wait until another day to finish up, as she was wont to do in the past.

"During my time in Australia, I had a wonderful, surprising opportunity because of a priest I knew back in America from Maryknoll, a society of priests and Catholic religious brothers and sisters that is dedicated to foreign missions, The opportunity was to accompany Mother Teresa on her journey through an area of the country where lived the aborigines, who were extremely poor.

"While we traveled there, she found a man who lived in a most terrible situation. She tried to talk to him to get him to allow her to clean his place up. Instead, he responded in a very brusque manner by saying, 'I'm all right!'

"He didn't realize he was speaking to a person of Mother Teresa's tenacity. She was once spit on when begging for money for the girls from the school she was working in at the time. Her response? She just said, 'Well that is for me. Now, what can you give me for my girls?' The man was so stunned that not only did he give her some support, but they also wound up becoming lifelong friends. She was amazing. At any rate, getting back to the story, she simply responded to his resistance by saying very firmly, 'You will be *more* all right if you allow me to clean up your place.'

"He wound up allowing her to do it, and during the process, she noticed he had a lamp. She asked him, 'Do you not light the lamp?' He responded, 'For whom? No one ever comes to see me.' Then he added very firmly again, 'I don't need to light the lamp!'

"Again, Mother Teresa was not put off. Instead, she retorted, 'If the sisters come to visit you, will you light the lamp for them?' He finally relented and said, 'Yes, if they come, I'll do it.'

"So the sisters put him on their ministry schedule and came to visit him regularly. And, as he had promised, he used to light the lamp for them in the evening when they arrived.

"Amazingly, despite the fact that he was not in great health, he lived for almost two more years, and I heard from one of the sisters who attended him and whom I had kept in touch with that at one point he sent back word to Mother Teresa through them, 'Tell my friend the light she lit in my life is still burning!'

"When I related this to the priest back at Maryknoll when I visited him in New York, he wasn't surprised. Instead, he encouraged me to remember the time spent with Mother and to use that memory as a beacon to show me where I should put my energies in the service of others. When I told him that working with people in pain just might not be my calling and that I might even feel God has abandoned these people, he nodded and said to me that social justice leader Jack Nelson once felt that way when he was in Calcutta. He got so upset, Father said to me, that he wanted to scream at God.

"In return, I asked Father, 'What did he wind up doing?'

"Father just smiled and said, 'He finally had the painful realization that, in his own words, "In the suffering of the poor, God was screaming at me."'

"Well, those are some of the touchstones of my calling. I am sure there are many more that determined psychiatry over some other helping profession. But those marked the beginning of my desire to help—not simply as a career but as a mission."

Kathleen could now sense that I was totally emotionally spent and really needed silence to reflect further rather than spending time on more stories, so she brought it to a close. "Jack, thank you for sharing all of this with me. Let's call it a day for now. Some other time, maybe we can speak about what you feel is at the heart of what you do psychologically. Maybe I could even speak about what may be the *spiritual* source of helping as well, if you were interested."

My face showed it all. Of course I would be interested. I knew she picked up my positive response because she then said, "Good. Let's look forward to that conversation. Good night, Jack."

"Good night, Kathleen...and thanks. This has been great."

Natural Compassion and the Circle of Grace

I had been invited to speak to a group of family practice physicians in another hospital in the city. I always loved to speak to this group because they were so in tune with the importance of self-awareness and presence to their patients. I guess this is why they chose family practice as opposed to one of the other specialties.

When I arrived, they brought me to a room where I could first relax and get my notes together. Before the organizer left me alone, though, he said, "Oh, by the way…," which is always the worse phrase you could hear as a speaker when you arrive with an expectation that you have a good sense of the type of audience you will face. He continued, "The director of the Surgical Residency Program said he wanted his docs to attend as well. I assumed that it would be fine with you and told him we would welcome their presence. Just wanted to give you a heads up."

After he left, I was in a foul mood over this change. I had dealt with surgical residents before, and they could be a tough group to address. Possibly it was because of the type of work they did, which required excellent surgical skills and an ability to focus on the anatomical rather than the personal aspects of their patients. Precision was the key, and I understood and accepted that...as I long as I didn't have to give a lecture to them!

As I was ruminating over this and complaining in my mind about the unfairness of the change, all of a sudden, Kathleen made her presence known with the question, "Why is this so upsetting for you?"

After I explained why I was both annoyed and hesitant now to present the lecture, she responded, "Are you prepared to speak on the topic?"

"Well, yes," I said.

"Then how they respond is irrelevant since you have no control over that. What you know you have control over up to this point is your preparation, which you have done. Now, what you do have control over is whether or not you are going to go into the lecture hall filled with the emotions you now have."

"Well, what would you suggest?" I asked.

"Recognize that if you have the space within you that comes from focusing on being a healing presence to them as well as delivering the content of your message, you will be able to put them at ease. If you focus on their possible resistance or on your own ego, that won't be possible, and it will defeat your giving them a place of inner peace in which they can spiritually rest for a while."

"You make it all sound so simple."

"It is," she replied. "But, once again, not easy. People don't easily realize it when they are caught up in their own desire to look good, accomplish something, or perform in a certain way. It is fun to succeed or be seen positively and applauded, but the most important message is to nurture a spirit within yourself based on faithfulness and trust in God, no matter what happens. Then, the chance will be good that they will catch that same spirit from you, which would be a great gift to them and one you are called to share."

I thought to myself, "That word 'calling' again."

She then left me alone to ponder what she had shared. I did and then quietly prayed for the gift of possessing and sharing this space of freedom and peace with those present. Following the encounters with Kathleen, myself, and in prayer, I went out and offered my comments in a more relaxed way because that is just how I felt. The surprising result for me? At the end of the day, I left feeling I had been present to the doctors in both the way I shared information and in the way I set the tone for them to feel as at ease as they could be.

Kathleen never brought up the incident again, but a wonderfully affirming event happened to convince me that she brought me the right message at a time when I was most open to hearing it—an important combination that therapists, mentors, and spiritual guides sometimes forget. A few days after the event, I received a call from the director of the Human Services Department at the hospital. She said she was sorry that she had missed my presentation, but her sister had been in the hospital, so she had needed to be at her side. After I asked about how her sister made out, she expressed gratitude for my interest and then switched gears.

She said, "Thank you for your kind inquiry about me and my sister, but the real reason I called is that a strange thing happened when you were here to speak."

"What was that?" I asked. She certainly intrigued me by this comment.

"Well, when I asked for feedback on your visit, those I could get to respond—because as you might expect, we are such a busy place that it is hard to track people down to ask them—those who responded said that they felt such peace in the room when you were here. It was as if you were so relaxed with them that they could also take a breath from their duties. The director of the Surgical Residency Program also said that he was surprised that all of his residents stayed for the whole day. They could have just as easily left after lunch or beeped themselves out on their cellphones during your presentations. I just thought you ought to know."

I realized at that moment that the grace of God was truly at work during that time. Kathleen had prompted me to embrace a new way of focusing on what I was to do rather than being so caught in myself. I was glad I responded as best I could. I did see that it turned out to be what I now call "natural compassion."

When I brought this up to Kathleen, she referred to it as taking part in a "circle of grace." When I asked her what she meant, she said, "You sought to bring helpful information, which, of course, you should. However, in your focus on them and not inordinately on yourself and a need for success or applause, you also provided an opening for them to experience the spirit of God. In turn, you have now been blessed in seeing that focusing on both faithfulness and sharing your inner spirit by giving people space turned out to be an awakening call to you once again to see compassion in a very different light. It is not simply doing something for others, as valuable as that is, but also being with them in a way that God may do what is possible with them through you at that moment."

Interestingly enough, it wasn't long before we spoke about this again. In doing this, obviously, Kathleen was letting me know this was quite important. The interaction with her and the positive outcome from my efforts to put into practice what was being taught to me, as in the case of any lesson, no doubt needed more than a single effort at practicing it before it would take root in me. And even then, there was no guarantee.

Observing myself when I felt negatively about something was a way I could see that the seed of a new spiritual perspective was falling on rocky ground at that moment. Only through attention to emotions such as my feelings of failure would the inner soil become rich enough for the lessons in natural compassion to grow—even amidst discouragement.

Discouragement was, I learned, yet another sign that once again I was centered on the wrong thing. This time I experienced it during a psychiatry course I was giving in Vermont for the psychology department at St. Michael's College. I always

loved doing these brief three-week programs because they were
not just a chance to share information and my philosophy of
treatment and mentoring but also it was a fine opportunity to
totally relax in a beautiful environment with great colleagues…
for the most part!

On one of these visits, I had an especially difficult interaction
with one colleague, who was also there to teach for the summer
at the School of Medicine at the University of Vermont campus
that was nearest to where I was located. I knew her from our
residency training program years ago, and I had consistently
experienced a similar pattern with her. She would be nice, and
when I would let my guard down, she would say something
quite unsettling. The intimacy of mutual respect was very hard
for her.

After this latest annoying interaction, I decided I would clear
my head by taking a walk by nearby Lake Champlain. It was a
gorgeous early summer Vermont day, and I didn't want to miss
a moment of it during my free time. As I previously alluded, I
was teaching a summer course that only required a few hours in
the classroom, so these periods were frequent and always a joy.

Even when it rained, I usually found a spot where I could stay
dry and still view the mountains. Such moments were *just right*.
At times like that, the low clouds and sweeping mist and occasional downpours made the scenery even greener. Then, when
the weather lifted, everything seemed so fresh and new again.
I felt like one of the first persons on earth, before people, cars,
machines, and the need to make money seemed to take away

from the gift of beauty God had planned and given to all of us if only we would take the opportunity to see.

This time, though, the environment around me couldn't quite dispel the dampened spirit within me. As I walked, I started to pose questions to myself that only made me more miserable: "Why wouldn't she listen? What were the reasons I couldn't help her?"

Following these questions, it didn't take long for my personal discouragement to once again turn into annoyance and anger: "If she remained so stubborn and couldn't see her role in things, didn't she know she was doomed to remain miserable and needy and keep pushing people away?"

Finally, I don't think Kathleen could stay silent any longer, and she burst out laughing which initially made it even worse. "Why are you laughing? This isn't funny. She is miserable, and because I handled it so poorly, I didn't make the situation any better...and now *I* feel terrible."

This time in a light, gentle voice she asked, "And, she did that to you?"

I think it was the way she asked it this time, more than the actual question, that freed me up a bit more to revisit my feelings to see what might be the cause of them. I knew the interaction didn't turn out as I would have liked it to; that didn't change. However, in the presence of Kathleen who seemed to want me to be both clear and kind with myself in the search for more wisdom, something shifted.

She sensed this new openness in me, so she pursued with other questions. "Do you think you did your best for her?"

"Yes. I feel I did."

"Well, then, just like in the case of the surgical residents you spoke to a while back, you were faithful to being compassionate. What did you expect would happen when you did this?"

"That she would see things differently and change."

"Good. On what did you base this expectation?"

And to this I honestly had to say, "I don't know. I guess it was what I had hoped would happen."

"That's understandable, but you don't want to be guilty again, as you have been taught by your Jesuit friend, of *the tyranny of unreasonable hope* do you?"

I became overly sensitive again and replied, "So, it was *me* who messed up, not her?"

I could tell Kathleen wasn't fazed in the least by my reaction when she replied, "No. Neither of you messed up. You did what you could at the time. She did what she could."

"So where does this leave us? Nowhere?"

"It leads us to recognize that walking alongside people experiencing difficulties isn't easy. As a psychiatrist, you know that sometimes we get ahead of them by seeking to be too direct with them. Sometime we fall behind when we are kind but not truly clear as to what we are seeing about them and their situation."

I still felt disheartened and said in a grumpy voice, "You would think that *as a psychiatrist* I would recognize that this listening and helping stuff is not easy—especially with people we know."

"No. It is not easy…but it is *simple*."

"What do you mean?"

"Remember when you told your mom that you helped a classmate who was feeling poorly. When she asked you what you did for her, you simply replied, 'I sat down next to her and helped her cry.'"

When I nodded in recognition of my own words and the attitude of simplicity back then, she added, "What we need to do is listen, reflect with them, offer any ideas, recognize that at the moment, for some reason, they can't respond to some of our suggestions, and then let God take care of what remains. Faithfulness, not success, once again is the goal. You know all of this as a psychiatrist because you deal with patients that are hard to reach. However, in your personal life, I think you would agree that it is not so easy unless you bring God into the equation more concretely."

I could feel her smile at me once again when she added, "You have some quiet time here which I know you enjoy. Take some of it, and reflect on what helps faithfulness, as I am suggesting, to take greater root." When I looked at where I thought she might be standing, alongside me by the lake, for more information on what she had just suggested, she didn't disappoint me.

"*First*, seek to have low expectations and high hopes that God will do something good with your encounters—not only with her but with all those people you find that you call, in psychiatric terms, 'resistant.'

"*Second*, forgive yourself and others for their defensiveness. As a psychiatrist, you know that this colleague wouldn't behave this way if she hadn't had some tough experiences early in life— ones she may not even remember or would deny if you asked her whether she did or not. She really is doing the best she can by trying to do what she feels is right, though she winds up doing self-defeating things that push away and annoy or hurt others instead.

"You also are doing your best, so picking on or having unrealistic expectations for yourself is tough on you and accomplishes nothing. As you know, it only fosters anger, self-recrimination, and discouragement. I have stood by your side when you lectured to new psychiatrists, psychologists, counselors, and social workers. You have told them that often in the short run their patients' negative style of dealing with the world is stronger than the therapist's health but in the long run, with patience, and I would add prayer, good outcomes can result."

Listening to her, my mind drifted back to a quote from poet W.B. Yeats that I took note of as a student and never forgot, "I have spread my dreams under your feet; Tread softly because you tread on my dreams." I needed to remember that when I dealt with persons I found annoying, seemingly rejecting of my help, needy, or ungrateful for anything done for them. I needed to remember the same with respect to myself.

Real hospitality was more than a group of techniques, setting out a good meal, or decorating the house before friends visited. It was deeply grounded in a welcoming relationship...*a circle of grace.*

Once at Christmastime, I decorated the house for a planned get-together with my brother- in-law, two nieces, and my parents. I spared no expense: The place looked like a ginger-bread house, the food and deserts were excellent—and both Aileen and Donna, I knew, loved sweets. I got special presents for everyone and made sure I left out nothing that the adults and children might want during my favorite season of the year. After it was all over, early in the evening, I also had a chance to take a walk with the girls down to the Ben and Jerry's store to get some Cherry Garcia ® ice cream to go with the pie.

Years later, Aileen emailed me when I was on an extended lecture tour of New Zealand and Australia. She recalled that special Christmas in the message, and I asked her in a return email what she liked best about it. Her amazing response—at least, amazing to me at the time—was, "When you held hands with Donna and me as we walked to the ice cream store that night. It was the first time since Mom's death that I knew deeply in my heart that even though she was gone, we wouldn't be alone."

When I shared that recollection with Kathleen as part of our discussion of compassion, her voice seemed to smile as she said, "When we let people into our spiritual homes for a momentary encounter or on a long walk to get ice cream, people get a chance to experience the peace of God. It reassures them that not only are they all right but also that they are not alone."

Since then, Kathleen and I have had many discussions and interactions around the spirit of compassion. I have begun to recognize that true loving is simple but again often not easy. We may do it, on occasion, out of guilt or duty. We may do it expecting gratitude or compliance in return. Rarely do we share freely and naturally expecting nothing in return. Jesus did that for us. Kathleen did it for me as my Guardian Angel. Now, I would like to do it more often for others. I knew I would often fail at it. Yet, it didn't seem to matter as much as it might have in the past. I also had another thing on my side: wonderful friends, even recent ones, who set the bar high for me in a good way.

Sometimes we experience the surprise of new friendship in a way that is quite unexpectedly powerful. A colleague of mine, for instance, told me that when he was about to become a psychiatrist, a good friend of his gave him Erich Fromm's book *The Art of Loving.* As a sculptor and a psychiatric resident, he wanted to give this person something special in return. And so he told me he had found a description in the book of someone who was quite a generous person. Then desiring to sculpt this person from simple pieces of wood from the university grounds to make a gift for his friend, he searched for the materials. He said to me that as he was looking around for just the right piece, an older fellow came up to him and asked if he had lost something. When he told him why he was searching, the man said, "Well, I am Erich Fromm. *Let's look together.*"

To be honest though, unfortunately, alongside such rare positive occurrences are more common dark ones. A tough piece to being compassionate with and kind to others is the danger in being close to the darkness in them that if we are not careful, can deflate us. Once when lecturing to persons finishing their psychology doctoral program, I tried to get the students to reflect on the flow of their day to see if they were living a truly balanced life. To accomplish this I asked what I thought to be a rhetorical question, "How do you spend your day?" But before I could continue after posing this question for their reflection, one student who had been working with addicts replied, "Helping people get through the night."

I realized at that point that psychologists, psychiatrists, people in ministry, educators, therapists, as well as parents, adult children of parents suffering from physical and mental disorders, and many of us concerned with the care of others don't have any infrared glasses that will help us find the certain path in the darkness. It is risky for everyone, and the spiritual ravines that mark the sides of the roads all of us take in life are populated with persons who didn't recognize the dangers of reaching out—especially if they do it without a solid circle of friends and a deep relationship with God.

With Kathleen's reminders at different points in my life, I have also tried not to forget that each encounter with another person was a potential circle of grace. If I simply reached out to others without also recognizing what lessons from God they were called to teach me, I would miss so much. Yet, in the end, as English writer Aldous Huxley once pointed out, "It is a bit embarrassing to have been concerned all one's life and find that at the end one has no more to offer by way of advice than: *Try to be a little kinder.*" How each of us does that may be different, but the basic desire to be gentle as well as clear in how we reach out to others and look at our own behavior, thoughts, and feelings is the same.

With Kathleen's continued help, I began less and less to depend on the hope of success with others. To be true, more often than I would like to admit, success often eluded me both in my clinical work and in some of my relationship with my colleagues, friends, and family. The blessing, though, was that more and more instead of focusing on success and being listened to, accepted or praised, I centered instead on being personally and professionally faithful. And, even more than that, I became interested in seeing not what I alone could accomplish, but with the theme of "low expectations and high hopes" held before me, I began to try to envision more and more what God might be doing with my efforts instead. Since I would never know totally, it was a mystery, a mystery I was getting more and more thrilled to be part of, no matter what the immediate results seemed to be.

I became so interested in all of this that quite surprisingly to me I was moved to write for the first time the following prayer that I decided to entitle *Lord, Am I Willing?* I'm not as good as I wish I was at writing prayers, but since over the years it has meant so much to me, I want to share it with you now.

Lord, Am I Willing?

Lord, am I willing to not rush to judgment about people whom I find tough to be with?

Lord, am I willing to set my expectations for others aside so I have room for hope that you will do something with them in ways I might not see?

Lord, am I willing to let people not like or understand me as I would desire but instead have the kind of patience with them that you continue to have with me?

Lord, am I willing to realize that compassion includes self-compassion?

Lord, am I willing to gently attend to my own inner life through spending some quiet time with you each day so I can share your presence with others by attentively listening to them rather than to my own needs at the time?

Lord, am I willing to be accepting of myself when I fail or become too concerned at times with my own image?

Lord, am I willing to really believe in the power of prayer so I am not sidetracked by my own fears, anxieties, desires for a quick solution, wish for appreciation, or aversion to negativity, trauma, and loss?

Lord, am I truly willing?

Help me to experience you in the midst of times when I encounter sickness, poverty, stress, anxiety, depression, misery, and sadness so I am not tempted to run away, harshly judge, or become depressed and helpless myself.

That is what I ask.

Amen.

When I finished saying this prayer for the first time, I could hear Kathleen softly say "Amen" as well. Although I no longer hear her say this anymore when I say this prayer on different occasions when I think God, and I, need to hear it, knowing she did say it that first time helps me remember that she is as close to me as is the Lord who created us both, and that feels good. *Very* good.

CHAPTER
TEN

SPIRITUAL SADNESS AND DARKNESS

The pickup truck Jaime used to ferry himself to the hospital when he was on call was in the shop, so I drove him to work. We were pretty much on the same schedule, so it was no big deal. At the end of the day, I surprised him when we met in the lobby and I asked him as we headed for the doctor's parking lot, "Would you mind driving?" He gave me a quick side look and said, "No problem," and smiled because he knew it drove me crazy when I thanked people for doing something and they responded that way.

When he didn't get a rise out of me, he asked as I was handing over the keys to him, "Are you OK?"

"Just distracted."

Then after we got into the car, buckled up, and pulled out, he said, "No. You look sad."

"Maybe I am a bit, but I can't seem to get in touch with it. Nothing major happened. A routine day. But somehow I started to feel low around mid-afternoon."

He waited, and when I didn't add anything in the next few minutes, he said, "You may have picked up the mood of some people you were treating or working with. It's natural. When I spend time with some of our 'brilliant' colleagues or members of my family, it can happen to me. It is not that they are depressed, but they just seem caught in neutral or constantly worrying about everything. I find it psychologically infects me until I am no longer my usual endearing, happy, funny, and incredibly attractive self." And at that, he smiled broadly.

I had to smile too and thought that was probably at least part of it. My patients didn't seem to have too much of a negative impact on me even when they were depressed. It was as if I knew enough by now to emotionally lean back a bit so I wouldn't join them in their negative frame of reference. However, with family, colleagues, and friends, it was a different story. I let them in, and if it was at a vulnerable time for me, it really put me in a gray place.

After we got to his place, he jumped out, thanked me for allowing him to be my driver, and told me that he hoped I felt better or at least could figure out what might be going on. "Might be something to learn with all of this," he said as he waved and walked over to his condo. But at the last minute he turned around and walked back to the car before I could drive off. When I saw this, I pushed the button to lower the window. He looked through the open window, smiled, and said in a gentle voice, "You know, Jack, even though you are a

psychiatrist, it is OK to feel sorry for yourself once in a while."
Then he walked away.

For some reason, his parting comment touched me more deeply than I might have expected, and I filled up a bit but when I got into the house. I thought I might avoid looking at the sadness and just putter around my little home library. However, I sensed this wasn't going to work because I felt the presence of Kathleen in the room as I was making myself a cup of coffee. It wasn't too long before she also said, "You seem a bit down."

"I am." I could even hear it in my own voice now.

"Did something happen?"

"Not recently."

"Then what?"

Instead of drawing a blank this time, all of a sudden a whole list of past failures came streaming in, and I told Kathleen this and started to share them. There was the time I yelled at a young neighbor when she jumped behind my car when I was getting ready to back up. My reaction made her cry. There was an act of cowardice committed on my part when I should have stood up for a friend but didn't. I remembered one of the times I put success or my own immediate enjoyment ahead of friendship and faithfulness. The list seemed to be endless. Because I trusted Kathleen with my inner recriminations, I went down most of the list and said afterward, "Shouldn't I be sad about all of that?"

Somehow I expected her to reassure me by saying that I was blowing things out of proportion, it was all in the past, and people make mistakes so stop picking on myself, but she didn't. Instead she said, "It's all right to be sad about your past mistakes." When I didn't say anything in response because I really couldn't think of anything, she let me be quiet with my own feelings of utter failure for a while and then softly explained to me about *spiritual* sadness.

"Everyone gets sad once in a while. Sadness is normal, and it can be good if you greet it in the right way. If you are honest, open, humble, seek to learn, and always, always, remember God is with you, alongside you, and will always love you, there is much to learn."

"So, guilt can lead somewhere?"

"No, not guilt. Guilt will just have you recall your sins and then psychologically beat up or defend yourself, and the only result is that it pulls you into the past and leaves you there. Nothing good can come of that."

"What then?"

"Remorse not guilt. Remorse will have you face your shortcomings or sins just as directly. You may even learn to always have your sins before you, but the result will be different."

"What's the difference?"

"Remorse will have you see what you have done wrong but not pull you into the past and leave you there. Instead, with God's love by your side, you will know you have done something wrong, face it, embrace it, and learn so you can be different in the present and the future."

She went on, "When this happens, sadness softens your soul, helps you become more humble, lets you be less harsh on others as well as yourself. It makes you see why you need the grace, forgiveness, and the goodness of God...once again, your sins and sadness *soften your soul* rather than drain or embitter you. In this way, you allow your sadness to become *spiritual* sadness because you have let God into your memory of failures, not kept God out."

Kathleen then went on to say, "So, you need to greet your anxieties, loneliness, regret, sadness, secret shame, loss, failings, sinful habits, *everything* that way. Instead of hiding things from yourself and God because they embarrass you, you also need to allow sadness to become something that brings you closer to the Lord. When you are neither hiding nor protecting yourself anymore, it can lead to a spirit of forgiveness of yourself as well as a greater inner freedom to become more intimate with God."

Although what she said was simple, we had partially gone over this ground before, and I felt I should know all of this, so at some level I felt stunned. I didn't know what to say, and she didn't say anymore. Instead, what came to mind, were Jesus's words which have since become my favorite, "I will not leave you orphaned; I am coming for you" (John 14:18).

Yet, after a few days, I did follow up on our conversation by turning the discussion this time to something that sounded like spiritual sadness but I had the feeling wasn't. "What you recently told me was helpful. I really could see that even fleeting sadness during the day can be a wake up call to learn something and is not simply a passing emotion to blow off or seek to quickly get over. It also keyed off something else in my mind."

"What was that, Jack?"

"It made me think of something I have heard about that sounds similar but I never fully understood: 'spiritual darkness' or 'dark night of the soul.'"

"Going into an intellectual explanation may not help at this point. What I think will help, though, is to understand that in spiritual darkness, as opposed to the lows of the day or severe clinical depression which you know all about as a psychiatrist, God is making new, different space for the divine presence within you."

She went on, "Up to this point, we have been speaking about your making space for God, and we should be addressing something as important as that. It is essential that you pray and be honest with yourself so you are well in tune with the movements of the Spirit during the day and throughout your life. However, part of your response must also be to recognize that in any relationship, God is acting as well."

"So, is there something I should do?" I asked.

"Some obvious things: When you feel a sense of dryness in prayer or, worse, a deep sense that God has abandoned you, rest in your prayer and know God has not left you. Let go during silence and solitude of a need to accomplish or change anything, and be especially attentive so you can notice God's surprising presence. Know that darkness may come and go at times, and above all, be patient and trust that God is moving through this change you are experiencing in ways that will deepen your relationship with him."

"In therapy, I can see when patients have an 'aha' moment and they are able to bear the fruits of these breakthroughs. What about in this case? Are there signs or fruits of a sense of darkness, dryness, or abandonment in prayer?"

"Yes, you will experience a strange paradox that will make you more determined than ever to meet God, even in, maybe especially in, the darkness. Also, you know a great deal about yourself already, Jack, but within the darkness you will go deeper in your appreciation of who you are, what your talents are, and where you trip over yourself—what you would call in your business 'defenses.' In addition, you will begin to become more creative because the impasse you are experiencing will not allow you to use your thinking left brain that you find useful in problem-solving by yourself and with your patients. In darkness, creativity and the right side of the brain will get the opportunity to open up if you are patient and remain faithful to prayer, your good work, and a desire for greater self-knowledge. With this, you will become more sensitive and peaceful, independent of external success, achievements, comfort, pleasure, or security."

I knew there would be so much more to learn on this topic, but as was often the case, I had the sense from the tone in Kathleen's voice as she ended her comments on darkness that it would have to wait for another day. I must admit that since I felt she had packed it in even more than usual on this occasion, this was a good idea. I would need to reflect on all of this and pray over it.

Experiencing a Little Bit of Heaven on Earth

In contrast to the sadness I just spoke about, I remember one morning waking up and feeling the sun on my face. It made me smile and relax as the night's sleep receded and I became more alert. It was a rare Saturday that I didn't have to go to work and hadn't lined up chores. I was free. I could also smell the coffee since I had one of those machines that I could set up the night before to perk at a certain time.

Slowly I got out of bed and walked into the kitchen to get a cup and sit down in the living room to relish the time even more. After I drew open the shades and sat down, my eyes were drawn to the little statue of a Scottie terrier I had outside the door. He was facing inside the back sliding glass door. He was out on the patio with his head tilted to the left side and had a look of yearning on his face. More than one person visiting would spot him outside on the patio facing in and say, "Oh, why don't you let that poor thing in? Look at his sad face, you meanie."

The little girl next door also loved the statue of the dog. When she was with her mother, she would just look at it. However, when she was with her easy-going grandfather, she knew he would let her do whatever she wanted, so she would pick up the statue and move him to different spots. I would find him facing in all directions at different places outside the sliding glass doors. Once, to make it even more fun, I piled up some stuffed animals I had from when my nieces were very young. They were stacked so they leaned against the back door facing the dog looking in.

The next time the little girl came around, I was lucky enough to be there and see her face. Her eyes got so big, and she smiled broadly and said to her grandfather, "Look!"

As all of this was going through my mind and I was sipping my coffee and smiling over it, I could suddenly hear Kathleen say, "That was a little bit of heaven experiencing the reactions of your young neighbor and feeling the way you did waking up, wasn't it? I am glad you didn't miss it."

"Heaven?"

"Yes, people often miss these episodes. There are so many occasions: a child laughing, an older person gratefully smiling while leaning on your arm as she struggles to walk, eating a piece of chocolate candy, hearing people sing a beautiful chant, feeling the energy of a busy city, walking quietly in the country by a lake, looking out over the water, doing a little good deed no one will ever know about…the list is endless. Yet, people miss it while looking for the spectacular. That's too bad."

While I felt grateful that I hadn't missed what she called "a little bit of heaven," I must confess that after hearing her comment I did wonder how many other "little bits" there were that I had walked by without noticing.

She seemed to recognize what I was thinking and said, "Good thing I brought this up for the future, eh?" I laughed because I was smart enough to know she was reframing my thoughts from being upset about what I had missed in the past to how I could be more sensitive in the future. I teased her, "Do angels always see the glass half full and not half empty?"

She laughed and in a playful voice said, "Yes, that's what we do!"

In what she said and how she reframed the picture for me, I truly recognized something important: that by having the eyes to see and the ears to hear, I could experience a bit of heaven in the ordinary events around, as well as experiences within, me. Yet, for this to happen, I knew I also needed to be more conscious of being grateful, and this would be another lesson for Kathleen to share with me.

One of my favorite writers when I was an undergraduate student was Rabbi Abraham Heschel. He often wrote on gratefulness and experiencing so much in this world that he felt God gifted us with if only we had the eyes to see. Shortly before his death, I remember reading that someone who was a friend, colleague, former student, and fellow rabbi said that Heschel told him that after he had experienced a heart attack, he woke up with no negative feelings. No despair. No anger. Only gratitude for the many miracles he had seen in his life. It was no surprise then that he wrote in a preface to one of his books that I was assigned for a course at Fairfield University in Connecticut that he never asked God for success, only for wonder and he felt God gave it to him. At the time, I thought, if only I could say that when I am ready to die.

In a comparative theology course from that same time at Fairfield University, I also came across the intertwined themes of awe and gratefulness again and again. One of them was among the sayings from the Ojibwa, one of the largest groups of Native Americans. It still echoes in a vague way in my mind. I think it went something to the effect, "Sometimes I go about in pity for myself, and all the while a great wind is carrying me across the sky." Again, if only I could appreciate that more fully instead of psychologically and spiritually pinning myself to petty grudges, concerns about my image, or aggravations about friends, family, colleagues, and patients who I find difficult, I would have a greater chance for inner freedom to welcome all that is around and in me that has been given to me by God.

As a psychiatrist, I have seen the different seeds parents have placed in the minds and hearts of their own children and grand-children that enable or hinder a sense of awe and gratitude. When I was playing with my niece Donna one day, there was a knock at the door. My brother-in-law, Bill, answered it, and one of the little neighbors stood in the doorway and made an announcement: "Life is a blank, and then you die!" She then said in a stage whisper, "The word isn't really 'blank,' but it is a bad word, so I am not supposed to say it." It was obvious she had heard it from one of her parents or older siblings. Already, this little girl was getting a message of defeat that said, "Do not expect or look for all the beauty God has in store for you."

The opposite side of this coin was Aileen, the other of my nieces, who always seemed to be brimming with a perspective on life marked by gratitude. One day I caught her staring out the window in the early morning as the sun rose and the sky was ablaze. She was all excited and screamed at me when she saw me standing in the doorway watching her, "Look, Uncle Jack, God is coloring the sky again!!"

If only she would continue to look that way at life, and if only I would begin to appreciate better the constant gifts that came and would continue to come before me as well. Not only would such an attitude be one of enjoying all God has given and continues to give me, but also I think it would add to my having a stronger spiritual life by absorbing a positive sense of God—one that not only would provide me with greater inner resilience but also one I could readily share with others in need along the way.

What Does Having a Strong
Spiritual Life Really Mean?

When having a conversation with Kathleen, somehow the experience felt like it was more than something similar to a telephone conversation with the unseen. Her presence was so palpable that it was more like a face-to-face interaction. During these times because she was so positive, I tried to model myself more after her and to keep the commandment *Thou shalt not whine*. Naturally, I often failed.

One of these times was after I heard a well-known speaker say very adamantly that all of us should have a strong spiritual life. As soon as I heard that for seemingly the thousandth time without any real guidance as to how to do it, I became really irritated and promised myself that as soon as I got home I would speak with Kathleen about it, and I did...or almost did. I didn't have a chance because she was waiting for me and made a preemptive strike as soon as I got in the door.

"I see you were graced this evening with a compelling urge to move from a general wistfulness about leading a fuller spiritual life to really acting on it in a way that your life will now become more of a pilgrimage rather than simply drifting from one activity to the other. That's wonderful."

"After hearing the speaker tonight, that's not exactly how I would have put it, but I like your reframing of my experience better than what it was when I heard him. I am still left, though, with the question I think many others have: What exactly does it mean to have a strong spiritual life? What do I need to do to enable this to become more of a reality?"

Kathleen waited a moment and said, "Well, who do you know in your life that you might ask?"

"Well, I am asking you."

"And that's fine, but I think you need to ask others in your life first."

I could tell she would not budge on this so pushing her further didn't make any sense. I also knew, at some level, that she was right. I needed to take some action in discovering a new way of life—the *spiritual* life, one that wasn't necessarily more "religious" but filled more fully with gratitude, awareness, and compassion. By asking me to find the answers, she was showing she had faith in me rather than me merely being dependent on her. Already, I had started to ferret the answers I was looking for. Now, who to speak to next?

I turned first to Suresh, or Fr. Michael as he was known in his parish, the priest who had been so helpful to me in my early life.

However, he must have taken a page from the "Kathleen Book of Guidance" because he didn't give me the answers either. Instead, he said, "You need a bouquet of answers, Jack. Not just some reflections by an old priest from India. My suggestion is that you visit the Carmelite nuns nearby." And he reached for a writing tablet and wrote down both the email address and the name of a contact person. "I will call her in advance and let her know that you are a psychiatrist interested in finding out different responses to what are the important elements of the spiritual life and that you want to interview the seventeen nuns who live there."

"You think she will allow such access?" I asked.

"Yes, I think she will. First, they are always willing to help for a good cause, and this is certainly one. Also, they owe me big time since they often have a hard time getting a priest for daily liturgy, and I usually help them out since I am retired now. Also, I am one of the few priests from India that they have as a celebrant who can keep his homily at Mass to less than ten minutes. For this they are even *more* grateful." And he laughed.

He then said, "Just give me a few days to get through to her. You should be good to go by next Wednesday unless you hear differently from me." I thanked him, and we went out for a nice long walk together.

When I didn't hear from him within the next few days, I went ahead and called Sr. Therese, the prioress of the carmel. As Suresh had promised, she was expecting my call and sounded enthusiastic. We set up a day and time for what turned out to be only an initial visit. It actually took eight mornings to be able

to speak to all of the nuns. With prayer, preparation for litur-
gies, work, quiet time, recreation, and meals, they were all a lot
busier than I ever suspected they would be as contemplatives!

I won't share with you now all of what they said. There would
be too much to include. Also, many of them retread the ground
of the others on certain aspects of the spiritual life that were at
the core of their lives, so I won't repeat their obvious love of
meditation, for example.

I was impressed by the great variety of ages, ethnic groups,
personalities, and levels of maturity of the nuns. Even in terms
of the place they held under the big tent called the *Catholic*
Church, I would find out in my interviews that there were those
who were very conservative, quite liberal, and what might be
referred to as middle-of-the-road in their outlook on church
doctrine. They did all have one thing in common though: a
passion for deepening their relationship with God and a deep
desire to help seed and grow it in others. I was very moved by
their commitment to both prayer and compassion—especially
in our modern stressful, competitive, often self-centered world.

One of the first comments that I heard was from a nun, originally from Vietnam, who had been there since shortly after she
finished high school. (She had spent one year working as a secretary for a local member of Congress.) She said straightaway,
"Doctor, as you look at the spiritual life, there are a couple of
things you need to take note of first."

"What would those be, Sister?" I could tell by the tone in
her voice and expression on her face that she was in serious

preaching mode because what she was to share was very close to her heart.

"One Protestant theologian, I forget his name, once rightly said, 'Jesus didn't call us to a new religion but to life.'"

"What do you think he meant by that?" I asked.

"He felt that sacred Scripture, all of the Church guidance or rules it comes up with, and whatever we believe or the Church teaches must lead to us to being more grateful for our birth and to our loving God and each other."

"Does that happen by our going to church or praying more?"

"Well, those activities should help us move in that direction, but without an attitude of faithfulness and openness, all the religious activities in the world would not soften your heart so you could hear the words of God. You would only mistake your own voice for that of the Lord."

When she said that, I immediately knew what she was talking about. I had been asked to see a seminarian once whom the rector of the seminary said quietly spent an hour each day in chapel. However, after he left the chapel after supposedly being in meditation for an hour, he came out and immediately spoke ill of other seminarians and the faculty. I also remember my sister, Sheila, asking me how she should handle one of the Catholic school mothers who went to daily Mass but would in Sheila's words, "cut you down at the ankles with her razor-sharp sarcasm and then walk away as if nothing had happened."

As I was recalling these two incidents, Sister, after pausing for a moment, added, "The faithfulness and openness that I am speaking about are especially important during the dark times of our life. To illustrate, I will tell you about my uncle who was a priest in the south of Vietnam, where most of the Catholics are in that country.

"Because he was a humble and good man—which many could see in how he lived his life with a sense of simplicity and generosity—people in the village were attracted to him. They went for counseling and support. They shared their secrets and hopes whether they were Catholic or not. He was a natural mentor because he had a welcoming attitude which is so rare even among helpers."

"What was that, Sister?"

"*Respect*. Even if he disagreed with you, he would look for the common ground between you. Even if he really felt he wanted you to follow what he would prefer, he always looked instead to what he felt the Gospel seemed to say about the difficulties you were going through. The Word rather than his preference— even if it appeared good to him—was the most important factor. People could see his selflessness and desire to be with them in the most difficult times.

"Well, what we would refer to here in America as the mayor became jealous of my uncle. So, he got someone to trump up charges against him. Once the claim was made, he was then marched through the street *naked* and beaten along the way by some of the mayor's cronies. It was terrible. But it backfired."

"What happened?" I waited for her next words.

"Well, people from the village, which was a long walk away, came to visit him in jail. Our sisters also came three times each day to provide food. The mayor was outraged, but what could he do? He knew if he did anything more, they would rise up, and he didn't want his superiors in Hanoi to hear of the event and see what he had done. And so, under such pressure, he finally released my uncle. In response, there was a celebration in the village at which my uncle was the guest of honor. He spoke briefly, but what he said really made all those present understand what 'the spiritual life' really means if we live it fully."

"What did he say?"

"He first focused on them by giving them the guidance they were so used to receiving from him in private. He said, 'In the darkness, we can experience the true Presence of God in ways we could never experience in the light, when things are going well. When I was imprisoned, one of the beautiful graces that came to the fore was the goodness of all of you bringing food even though you had to walk such a long distance and needed to leave your crops at harvesting time. True generosity is a reflection of the Holy Spirit's presence in the world.

"'Another grace,' he said, 'was the strength God gave me to be open and faithful to what was really important—not my freedom, not my reputation, not even my physical well-being. Only my identity as a child of God was essential. God welcomed me even closer when in my nakedness and imprisonment I might, without my faith, have felt so alone, unnecessarily ashamed, and embarrassed.'"

At this point, Sister became quiet and looked as if she was revisiting the events that took place and sitting for a moment again next to the side of her uncle. As in the case of my time with Kathleen at times or during quiet moments in my clinical practice, as I was trained to do, I remained silent as well. I was not simply waiting for my opportunity to speak or for another comment to be made but instead I sought to process all I had just heard. I didn't want the essence of Sister's message to elude me because I could intuitively sense how important it was. I also wanted to be in solidarity with her at this recollection of a very poignant and teachable moment in her family history.

She finally looked up, smiled, and said, "People often speak about 'the spiritual life' when they feel they don't have one or are lost as to what it means. What it means is living fully, opening ourselves up to all that is going on around and in us in a way that welcomes new learning and finding new ways to be compassionate. I guess that is why we pray. A friend of mine who is a dean of a seminary once said, 'People live cautiously because they pray cautiously.' I think those of us who live here at the Carmel know that, and for that reason we wish to pray so we can be on the adventure we call 'the spiritual life.'"

With that she got up, smiled, gave me a hug, and walked out. I felt she had taught me a great deal. She also left me with a profound question to tackle: *What really is prayer?* It took me the next six visits with the nuns to figure out to some degree an answer to that question which would be comprehensive, life-giving, challenging, and, of just as great importance even though it might not sound like it, practical.

WHAT IS TRUE PRAYER?

Since Sister had opened up the door for me to finding out what prayer might actually involve, I was eager to open up additional time to return to speak with more of the nuns. In the case of the next Sister I would speak with, the beginning was not what I expected it to be.

"So, you are interested in the spiritual life and prayer? I am pleased for you that you are asking those questions. It is a good sign for you because it means that God is chasing you. Otherwise, you would not have been given the gift of inquiry into these things." With a broad smile on her face, she then added with emphasis, "You are *very* lucky."

This was not the first time I had heard that. Still, hearing her say that was like an arrow shot through my arrogance. I thought I was the one who should be commended for seeking to have a stronger spiritual life. Instead, she was telling me that, of course, I should be thanking God for giving me this desire.

Wait until I shared this with Kathleen! Knowing me as well as she did, I knew she would especially love it. I could hear her saying with a bit of a tease in her voice, "A humble psychiatrist? What next?"

Sister continued, "Prayer, if it is true prayer, is evident in the fruits of peoples' behavior. In how they enjoy the gift of their life and share it freely with others. A good example of this is Sister Edith who is now ninety-two. You can see it in how she enjoys all her food. She eats very slowly, intentionally, and with real appreciation. I guess that is one of the reasons why she never overeats and is so thin. You can also see it when she drinks a martini or glass of wine."

"She drinks? At ninety-two? That's OK?"

"Well, if you were to ask her if she was a drinker, she would say, 'I am a dedicated drinker, you know. I drink three glasses a year without fail.'"

I was now totally puzzled. "What does she mean?"

"She has a martini on her birthday. It takes her two hours to finish it while she is eating the snacks she rarely eats during the year. She also has a glass of white wine after the Easter Vigil and a glass of red wine at Christmas dinner—red, she says, because it is the color of the season."

"She doesn't drink other than that?"

"No."

I forgot temporarily about prayer and asked, "Do other Sisters drink? Any have problems?"

She didn't seem to think my questions were irrelevant or intrusive, so she quickly responded, "Several will have a drink now and then, especially during the holidays. Most don't bother."

"See any with a problem?"

"Not really. A few had problems before they entered, but when they came here, they were already nondrinkers. We did have one middle-aged woman who wanted to join us, but we noticed she would drink almost every night. We could see that was a sign she was not coming to join our life but to try to avoid hers. We did the pastoral thing by not trying to fix her but encouraged her to get the help she needed so she could first live life on the outside fully before eventually coming here to see if our life is what God and she wanted."

Her response was such a psychologically sensible one that I had to stop for a minute to regroup. More often than I would like to say, I would be requested by a religious congregation to treat a woman who said she wanted to become a nun. I am not sure why they did it in such needy cases. Maybe they felt it was the kind or pastoral thing to do. Maybe those in charge of spiritual formation or community leadership thought it was important since the numbers were low. Usually I wound up showing them that a pastoral diagnosis was essential so the treatment would be correct or truly what they were terming "pastoral."

What that meant is if the person needed a great deal of help from the start, it usually meant that religious life was not for her, at least at this point. It was not a good idea because the group of Sisters she wanted to join would wind up spending an inordinate amount of time trying to accommodate her need—usually without success and to the detriment of the psychologically healthy or emotionally marginal nuns already in the community—rather than focusing on what they were called to do and be. I usually needed to convince the congregation's leadership or their vocation director that, bottom line, religious life was supportive and communal but *not* meant to be a therapeutic community. Sometimes I succeeded in this; sometimes a mistaken Catholic ethos of 'chronic niceness' won out, and the problem remained and unfortunately only continued to get worse. Sad. And to my mind, usually, with some consultation, avoidable.

Sister seemed to be pondering what to say next to me. Finally, she said, "From hearing about your interest in prayer from the nun you have already interviewed, I must admit that I find it refreshing."

"How so?" I asked.

"Well, many people are expecting prayer to be like learning magical words to use when either they are feeling down or they want to ensure they are not going to be punished after they die. You seem to be seeking something more. It is like the spiritual life for you is something you want at the core of your daily activities so you don't miss the numinous and can share it in a way that is natural rather something done out of some other motivation. At least that is what Sister seemed to relate to me of what she sensed about you."

While I didn't feel she was wrong, I recognized how intuitive the previous nun had been. Some of what she sensed about me was not in my questions but possibly in the way I had asked them—namely, with a sense of real desire as to how I could come fully alive. I just didn't want to miss my life or fail for some unknown and avoidable reason to share it freely with those around me. I did want the Holy Spirit to come, no matter what it took.

She went on, "What prayer does is it helps you to rejoice in who you are, look at both your gifts—which you need to know fully if you are to enjoy and share them—and your sins so you can see under what circumstances you are getting lost for the moment. Prayer should help you be a person who also values innocence. It should help you be transparent and seek to find God in *everything*—your happy times, your faults, the troubles that might find you or you get yourself into, illness, pleasure… well, *everything*."

From what I have told you thus far, you can see how I would agree with her, but I still asked "How does prayer do this?"

I think she sensed I wasn't getting into my head in asking this because she nodded and went on. "Well, when we are quiet during meditation or hear a homily, there are many responses the world would have us take. We might become zoned out— run away for the moment—or start picking on ourselves or blaming others. We may get discouraged or distracted by desires, compulsions, or something else that is irrelevant. Instead, prayer is being aware, what in your business they might call 'being mindful.' To do this, you need to be attentive and interested by all that is around and happening within you so you can see where God is leading you next."

Sister was obviously not simply prayerful. She was very bright, had read on psychology, and knew people well including, I imagine, herself.

"To help make this possible," she went on, "prayer involves a structure that is not meant to constrain us or be something artificial, but to the contrary," and she paused for a few seconds, "it is designed to help us truly be awake like the apostles at the transfiguration. They would have missed it if they were physically or, more aptly today, psychologically asleep.

"So before we stop, because we soon have midday prayer, let me at least check off some ways to pray so you can think about them before you come back to visit us again. Prayer includes:

Paying attention to our emotions. They often tell us 'who our god is.' Jesus once said, 'Where your treasure is, your heart is.' Our emotions will tell us what we are inordinately concerned about.

Making use of the crumbs of alone time when you are by yourself and quiet or simply reflective in a group. Doctor, look during the day to see when and where you can find a bit of silent space.

Reading the Old and New Testament in a way that makes you feel part of the scene. See what strikes you and what questions God may be asking you as you read the stories and seek to understand the parables. Too often people's faith becomes too vague because they have lost connection with God because they no longer read the sacred Scriptures.

Going to Mass to encounter God in the Eucharist, in the Word (epistle and Gospel) as it is broken open, and in those other worshippers present.

And, reflecting mentally or writing down at the end of the day what you feel about what has happened and, in light of what you believe, what God may be teaching you.

She took a breath after providing this list and ended by saying, "That ought to get you going, eh?" And we both laughed.

After leaving Sister, I remembered that Kathleen had once said prayer was an attitude and activity that helped us notice God in our life in ways that would awaken us to what *all* of life could be—even in the gray and dark times. Sometimes I would find that what she said was correct in even little ways.

For instance, when I went to one church in India while I was providing some lectures at two of the medical colleges, just prior to remembering Christ with the words, "This is my Body…This is My Blood," the celebrant of the Mass first took off his shoes as a sign of respect. His acknowledgment of what was about to happen to the bread and wine in front of him and that he would soon be in the physical presence of God in a unique way, would be on holy ground, caused him to want to confirm his awe at this important event. It surprised me and opened my eyes, possibly for the first time to that degree, to the tremendously significant event that would soon take place. That prayer and our prayerful actions can open our eyes even wider are two spiritual realities that came to mind later on when I had a chance to fully reflect on what had occurred.

My interactions with Kathleen, Suresh, the Sisters, and so many others made me not only want to pray but to understand and experience it more deeply. I didn't want to see it any longer as simply asking God for things. I wanted my prayers of gratitude, requesting, rejoicing, confession, and confusion to be real. I realized I now wanted my encounter with sacred Scripture to translate into a new way of encountering my own life and the lives of others. I didn't want prayer to make me feel more 'religious' or happy. I wanted nothing less than to be alive with God.

As I put the above words in my journal, I recalled a few lines I had written a month or so earlier in the little diary I had bought for my notes. The words were from my new friend Henri Nouwen's book *Making All Things New*. After leafing around for a moment or two, I found them again. They read, "The beginning of the spiritual life is often difficult not only because the powers which cause us to worry are so strong but also because the presence of God's spirit seems barely noticeable. If, however, we are faithful to our discipline, a new hunger will make itself known." Thank God. It was doing just that now for me.

I then went on to read more of what Henri had said about the hopes of such a dramatic response to God's call to be open to new divine experiences in our lives and the promises it offers:

> What is new is that we no longer experience the many things, people, and events as endless causes for worry, but begin to experience them as the rich variety of the ways in which God makes his presence known to us. When our hearts are set on that kingdom, our worries will slowly move to the background because the many things which made us worry so much start to fall into place.

As a person deeply interested in the spiritual life, these words touched me quite personally and deeply. So much so, in fact, that even though I was in way over my head and a beginner at prayer (and always would be for that matter), I wanted to summarize what I felt I knew about the spiritual life now, so I did.

Some of what I came up with that I didn't want to forget at this point included unexpected opportunities to encounter the presence of God in "places" such as my negative emotions; memories; preoccupations and worries; during illness or when I felt bored; at times of discouragement; when I am tempted to rush around during the day; when there is a significant change or loss in my life; when people inspire me to act and I do... or, for some reason, don't; when I feel patient and am more appreciative than usual; and spontaneously when I gently understand instead of judge others harshly.

All of this seemed to be going in the right direction. These themes were in line with my wanting to prioritize the God-relationship in my life. Yet, if I were to do this, I knew I would have to be even more honest. I would have to uncover what truly often represented "the psychological and spiritual center of gravity" in my life that was taking most of my attention and that I was making into a god. In accepting this challenge, I knew Kathleen was right once again. This wasn't going to be so easy after all.

FINDING YOUR SPIRITUAL CENTER OF GRAVITY

I often try to find stories that I can share with my patients, and especially in the case of adolescents, ones that they can easily remember and apply during a difficult challenge. In this way, they could more readily be aware of the point I made in therapy or mentoring to encourage greater psychological health.

Following my early visits to see the nuns at their Carmel, one of the last things I had heard from the Sister teaching me about prayer was her quoting Jesus as saying, "Where your treasure is, your heart is." It reminded me of the story I used when I wanted people to know that their own role in letting go of something was crucial to their moving ahead in therapy. It was a story of how one group of people learned to catch monkeys:

In Africa, there were a group of trackers who would go into the jungle to catch monkeys to sell to zoos and animal collectors around the world. They would do this in a very calculated way. First, they would find gourds and cut off the large end so they could hollow it out. Then after emptying it, they would fill it with peanuts. Once filled, they would then reattach the large end and then cut off the small end this time. Following this, they would attach the gourd to a tree and leave.

Once the trackers left and it became quiet—you could tell by the fact that the birds no longer sounded alarming shrills—the monkeys would feel safe enough to come down and see what the humans had done to their territory. When they did this they found the gourds, looked into them, and both saw and smelled the peanuts. In response, they would then reach into the gourd to grab the peanuts.

As long as they held onto the peanuts, they could not get their hands out. All they needed to be free was to let go of the peanuts, but many of them would not. The result was that they remained in the jungle, holding on, screaming in frustration and eventually fear until the trackers came back, captured them, and took them to a zoo or place of captivity where they would be imprisoned for the remainder of their lives.

The obvious question and ultimate lesson in telling this story is: What are we holding onto that is making us miserable? What are we inordinately centering ourselves on or demanding as a price of our happiness to the detriment of all that is around us as gifts to enjoy and share with others?

Although this question was important to me and those I sought to help from a psychological vantage point, I now realized it had an even more deeply spiritual dimension: Who or what was I making my god? No matter what I said I believed about God, who or what was really preoccupying and worrying me? What was I spending my days getting myself crazy about or desiring?

What Jesus said made complete sense: "What's the use of worrying. How can you change anything one iota by doing that?" He wasn't simply saying to stop wasting your energy on what you can't control. He was also saying, as I could see it, let go of everything—including those things and people you wish you could control—so you can be open to enjoying as much of the life I have given you so, in turn, you could freely share it with others. It was very much in line with a phrase from the Talmud that one of my Jewish colleagues once shared with me when I spoke with him about a devoutly Jewish patient who was fearful of enjoying his life and so was, in turn, driving his family crazy. He told me it was written in the Jerusalem Talmud that when we die, God will hold us responsible for all the gifts we were given in life that we didn't enjoy.

Prayer, I now knew, would help me recognize when I, myself, was not doing that. Through this intentional practice, in order to have my hands free to greet and celebrate life once again, I could repeatedly let go when I caught myself holding on.

As I took more and more time in silence and solitude, I began to see all that was contaminating my mind and crippling my heart. As I took a few moments in the morning after reading some Scripture for the day, I would do this by first leaning back in the chair in order to quietly stare at an icon of the holy family. Gently, I would then breathe in and out and utter the word "peace" in my mind. Time and time again, episodes I wished I could forget, people I was annoyed or angry with, desires that I had, chores to be done, and other thoughts, wishes, fears, and negative concerns came to mind during the time I did this.

Rather than being viewed as my prayers simply being filled with distractions, they were now showing me what I was holding onto. Morning meditation was helping me uncover those things that were dominating the music playing in my heart throughout the day without my awareness. In quiet prayer, though, the space was there to hear it whereas before I was too distracted with the noise of the day. As suggested by one of the nuns and confirmed by Kathleen in one of our later chats, I didn't entertain the thoughts but neither did I try to suppress them. I knew the only memory that could hurt you is the one forgotten because it stayed around beyond your awareness pushing you to think and behave in ways that weren't helpful. As I meditated and considered the spiritual aspect, I now knew that if I could let them move through me like a train while I sat with a loving God, they would change. They would take their proper place, be seen for what they were, and settle like dust so I could see clearly, feel stronger, and behave more justly.

Composer Arthur Rubinstein once quipped that "happiness can only be felt if you don't set any condition." Prayer helped me see the very conditions I was setting for my happiness:

I must be promoted.

She must respond successfully to my treatment.

My family needs to more clearly appreciate my needs.

Money must be there so I can buy what I want when I want.

Good health should always be present.

People must respect what I do and give me credit for it...constantly!

I must be viewed favorably.

The list was endless. It was as if I were living with the belief that when my needs weren't met it was tantamount to a sacrilege. I was almost claiming that God had made a pact with me that my life should be without concern, physical pain, emotional discomfort, or spiritual hunger. As I focused more and more on my prayer and the theme of letting go, I began to realize that although I can grow in psychological health and depth in my prayer, there was no such thing as a spiritual retirement. It would always be a journey in letting go and seeking a more dynamic prayerful relationship with God. Kathleen had and would continue to teach me this in many ways, but one of the primary avenues I was to find was through a greater understanding of what is referred to as "desert wisdom."

HONORING MODERN DESERT WISDOM

Because I am a bit of a history buff in general, I became interested in the events that formed the early Church as well. In my reading about it, and I must be honest, I have only begun a survey of what has been written by church historians, I became aware of the desert fathers and mothers, the *abbas* and *ammas* of the fourth and fifth centuries. I could tell from some of my interactions with Kathleen that she had a special place for these men and women who took their faith so seriously. And so, one afternoon when I was relaxing in a friend's cabin on Lake Champlain, just outside of Burlington, Vermont, I decided to broach the topic with Kathleen—especially since I had brought a couple of books for spiritual reading that were on this subject: Thomas Merton's *The Way of the Desert* and Henri Nouwen's *The Way of the Heart.*

So, I said to her, "I've read and you have shared a little bit about the desert fathers and mothers. Could you give me a bit of a better sense about them? What is the most important thing I should know? I have a feeling there is something much more to learn and emulate, but I don't want to simply be like a misguided anthropologist digging in the wrong spot while just next to it are the true spiritual artifacts. The reason I mention all of this is that two sections from the Merton and Nouwen books intrigued me enough to ask further about them."

"What did they say in them?" she asked.

I had the books both next to me on the glider on which I was sitting, so I reached over and picked up the Merton book first. "Merton wrote: 'These monks insisted on remaining human and "ordinary." This may seem to be a paradox, but it is very important. If we reflect a moment, we will see that to fly into the desert in order to be extraordinary is only to carry the world with you as an implicit standard of comparison. The result would be nothing but self-contemplation and self-comparison with the negative standard of the world one had abandoned. Some of the monks of the desert did this, as a matter of fact: and the only fruit of their trouble was that they went out of their heads. The simple men who lived their lives out to a good old age among the rocks and sands only did so because they had come into the desert to be themselves, their ordinary selves, and to forget a world that divided them from themselves. There can be no other valid reason for seeking solitude or for leaving the world.... Moreover, they knew that they were helpless to do any good for others as long as they floundered about in the wreckage. But once they got a foothold on solid ground, things were different.'"

Kathleen said, "Yes. I could see why that section struck you as being helpful and revealing of who they were and what they were modeling for us. What did Henri write that was of help?"

"He wrote, 'The world they tried to escape is the world in which money, power, fame, success, influence, and good connections are the ways to self-esteem. It is the world that says, "You are what you have." This false identity gives the security and safety which we are searching for, but throws us in the spiral of a permanent desire for more—more money, more power and friends—in the illusion that one day we will arrive at that dream place where nobody and nothing can harm us. The hermits of the desert were deeply conscious of the fact that not only the society but also the church had been corrupted by this illusion.... They escaped into the desert to free themselves from this compulsive self, to shake off the many layers of self-deception and reclaim their true self.... The way of the *abbas* and *ammas* of the desert makes it clear that finding our identity is not the simple result of having a new insight. Reclaiming our true self requires a long and often slow process in which we enter more and more into the truth."

I said, "I think Nouwen was saying that their stories and sayings—again in his own words—'can speak directly to us, who live at least fifteen centuries after they were first written down. They do not require much explanation. What they do require is a spirit of discipleship, that is, a willingness to listen, to learn, and to be converted...'"

After that, I put down the two books and gazed out over the lake. Kathleen always seemed to appreciate my need for silence after I had spent time trying to absorb some key spiritual message, so probably for the hundredth time at this point, she gave me the space to be with what I was seeking to absorb. Finally, when I noticed one of the ferries out in front of me traveling from Colchester, Vermont, across the lake to New York, my reverie was broken.

Soon after, she seemed to sense this and spoke: "I had an early introduction to the lives of the desert mothers and fathers since I had the opportunity to be a spiritual companion—what you would call a Guardian Angel—to one of them."

"Really?" I always forgot that while Kathleen was my guardian angel now, as she had once shared with me in passing, she had been "on the job" for centuries. "Who was it?" I asked.

"Amma Syncletica. A truly amazing woman. But first let me share with you something about the times and what went on because some people misunderstand the movement and its imperfections. Then I want to share with you some of her words. Taking them with you and keeping them as a prayerful nest within while you are here in Vermont is a good start, I think."

She then went on, "As maybe you have already read in the two books you brought, what precipitated the movement by some to the desert was that the emperor at the time decided that Christianity, which up to that point had been forbidden, was now to be permitted. When this happened the Church that was so challenging of the culture of the day up to this point ran the great risk of becoming part of that very secular culture itself. Some in the Church felt they needed to go off to the desert so as not to be influenced in a way where they would fail to center their lives on what was truly important—God, their faith.

"Many who stayed and didn't go away to experience silence, solitude, or a community of prayer in the desert were still able to remain faithful. Also, on the other hand, some of those who did go off to the desert, as Merton said, didn't remain faithful to God. They simply did something they felt was spectacular as a way of being special, and it didn't have a good impact on them or on those with whom they interacted.

"The good that did happen was that in journeying to the desert some found a sense of simplicity, a greater opportunity to see how much they relied on God, and an appreciation of work as a form of prayer since they were mindful of God as they did it. And so, because of all this, they not only often became more spiritually centered, they also became freer to serve others."

She stopped at that point, and I had a chance to reflect and comment. "I understand the part about simplicity, reliance on God, and a new appreciation of work as a form of prayer. I think when I am mindful during a psychotherapy session, I feel the presence of God and understand the role of grace because I can be prepared as a psychiatrist but can't effect the healing. What I don't fully understand is why they became freer to serve others."

"Well, firstly, hospitality is essential in the desert. Surviving without others is close to impossible. Secondly, they learned to live more graciously without unnecessary worries or desires to go down fruitless paths because the temptations just weren't there in that way. However, of most importance is that in seeking to not fall prey to the culture of greed, power, and preoccupation with one's image, as well as become too concerned about security, possessions, or successes, they became freer within. If they were truly in the desert alone with God and not their ego, if they were honest with themselves and open to listen to God and not their own opinions, what often occurred is that their self-knowledge and deep sense of God became greater. As a result, when they were with others, without holding onto the illusions and delusions upon which their identity had been previously based, they were more apt to be, as we have spoken about before, persons without guile who could purify the air for the rest of humanity—including those who came to receive a word from them."

"A *word*?"

"Yes, many came to the spiritual mothers and fathers of the day to receive a saying or word to help them find the richness of their lives and share it with others or, to term it differently, find God and be truly compassionate. If you continue to read Merton's book on the *abbas* and *ammas* you will see he included sayings from that period. Nouwen has included them in his book as well, and Benedicta Ward, who is the premier scholar on the topic, has a whole array of them."

When she said this, I remembered again that Kathleen also came across as a desert mother—extremely wise and talented and certainly someone without guile—to me, and she knew so much from early history right through contemporary times that I was constantly amazed at both her knowledge and wisdom. Given this, I was distracted at this point during our conversation by the thought: "Gosh, I am so lucky to have her in my life." However, whether she knew what I was thinking or not, neither of us commented on it.

After being delayed by this thinking for a moment, I finally was able to ask, "What should I start with?"

"Begin with the appreciation that the *ammas* and *abbas* sought a God whom they were called to find in a way no one else could. They could not accept someone else's formulation. They needed to pray with that conviction."

"Yes. I think that is a beautiful way for me to begin."

After saying this, I could feel my emotions rising to the surface. I had taken the time off because I was so tired from keeping such a crazy schedule, and my nieces seemed to be having a hard time since the anniversary of my sister's death was coming up in a couple of weeks, so I knew that was taking a toll on me as well. Yet, I think my emotions were showing on my sleeve because when Kathleen used the word "prayer," it struck me more deeply than ever before. I felt I wanted to pray, but it still seemed so hard for some reason.

She seemed to sense this, as she often did when I felt something deeply in my soul, so she added, "Maybe the following quote from Amma Syncletica—a 'word' she gave to someone who came to her with a desire to be closer to the Lord but felt stymied—would help. I once heard her say to a young woman who said she was having a hard time in prayer, 'In the beginning there is a struggle and a lot of work for those who come near to God. But after that there is indescribable joy. It is just like building a fire: at first it is smoky and your eyes water, but later you get the desired result. Thus we ought to light the divine fire in ourselves with tears and effort.'"

As I was absorbing the *amma's* word to the young woman and now, centuries later, to me, I could sense Kathleen was ready to let our conversation move into silence and to allow me to feel the solitude of the moment. I didn't feel left up in the air with this. The timing was right for me to sit quietly alone with God now as I gazed again over the lake. I knew we would talk about the desert again—both the historical one and the ones I would enter—and knowing that relaxed my grip on the topic. It was also time to quietly simply be and let that very space open me up to God in a new way for now and lead me into the immediate future as well.

By the afternoon of the next day, although I had the opportunity to walk by the lake for quite a bit of time, I was also still able to finish reading both the Merton and Nouwen books since they were fairly compact in size. In addition, after rereading what I had underlined, I put some notes in my journal that I want to share with you now.

One of the main tasks I felt that the desert dwellers believed they had to undertake was to find out what they were filled with in terms of desires as well as to uncover what they were focusing on that wasn't helpful. They did not want to be slaves to what others often were so they could be free within to experience life and share it with others in a generous way. To accomplish this they found they would require a much greater *trust in God* than they had experienced in the past. One of the stories I read which brought this to mind, I wrote out by hand in my journal so I wouldn't forget it. It was written by a young desert disciple.

> One day when Abba Bessarion and I were walking along the sea, I became very thirsty and shared this. In response, the elder prayed and then told me to drink from the sea. I did, and the water was sweet. After I finished, I poured some into a flask so I would not be thirsty later on in the day. Seeing this, the old man asked me, "Why are you doing that?" I responded, "Pardon me, Father, it is so I won't be thirsty later on." To which he responded simply, "God is here; God is *everywhere.*"

As I read that story, I realized how self-reliant most of us tend to be. In many ways, this is good. However, I could feel now that there was a danger in it as well: to forget that our gifts are all from God—including the divine treasure of so many people in our family and circle of friends who, so we don't forget, are also deserving of credit for what we have and who we are today.

I was glad Kathleen had also directed me to the writings of the desert fathers and mothers because I could now see better that part of the holding on process for me, on a deeper level, also included my sometimes being inordinately filled with a sense of crippling entitlement and self-righteousness when I didn't get what I felt I deserved or people didn't behave in the way *I* thought they should.

So, the question for me at this point that seemed to pervade the different approaches to recognizing where I had settled for less than the freedom and graciousness of God centered on one word: *humility.*

Would I be open enough to Kathleen and to my own and others' efforts at raising my awareness to those areas in which I was enslaved? Since I was so entrenched in my own habits and the hidden chains of my own preoccupations and opinions, would I even be able to unearth my almost hidden values, characteristics, and ingrained approaches to myself and life? As I pondered these questions, a Chinese proverb, written in the form of a question, that I had written down as a result of other reading I had done a while back came to mind in terms of myself: "Does he have too many tics to feel the itch?" A disturbing thought—at least for me—then came to the forefront: Would my ingrained personality, traits, and habits prevent me from *ever* being free?

I knew some of the signs or resistances to letting go. Also, these were supplemented by what I had just read in the books on desert wisdom on the hesitation to jump into the darkness with God.

What I felt I needed to do at this point to keep moving ahead was to write down what I knew intellectually so I could bring it up in prayer by reviewing my journal during quiet times. My sense was that it would help me absorb its power a bit more as a way of confronting my own resistance to change. At least that was the hope. Also, I thought it would serve as a good way to discuss with Kathleen some difficulties in my journey toward freedom, God, and greater compassion for others.

The first theme that came to mind was the very specific question: What am I focusing on most in my life? Who or what am I making into an idol? I knew this would be tricky, but if I was willing to pick up what preoccupied me much of the time and could see more clearly the things I resented when my desires were not fulfilled as I would like them to be, I could learn much by bringing them to prayer and sharing them with those who held mentoring roles for me.

Another avenue to finding out about my resistances was unearthing the one thing I had convinced myself was necessary for my happiness. I knew this also was going to be hard because this often involved good things. For instance, my concern about my two nieces, Aileen and Donna, and brother-in-law, Bill, was good. However, worrying about them would not only waste energy, it could prevent me from being a healing presence when I was with them.

I knew this for a fact because a couple weeks back I had heard that one of the girls had to deal with a bully again at school. I was so upset and angry about it because Aileen was such a nice, gentle girl. When I finally showed up at their house to supposedly support her, she could visually see I was upset when I spoke with her about it. Finally, she laughed a bit, and said, "Uncle Jack, you look worse than I feel when you speak about the bully." When I heard this, I knew once again that when something gets me upset or moody if it doesn't go my way, it is a red flag that I am not letting go. In the case of my niece Aileen, if I had been willing to let go of my own feelings of helplessness, I could sit with her more helpfully to aid her in her own sense of feeling weak and possibly embarrassed. Instead she wound up supporting me!

Thinking about this also helped me to recognize that many of my negative or unhelpful responses that occur when things don't go my way are practically automatic. Yet, I must admit reading the books on desert wisdom as well as receiving Kathleen's constant optimism made me still feel that freedom and emptiness would open up for me if I were willing to face the questions and comments I had written in my journal. I had hope about my prospects.

I knew that with prayer, effort, and guidance I would feel calmer, better able to take life and myself more lightly, and, as a result of this, be freer for those whom I loved and served. I did not delude myself that it would be easy. To grow in spiritual freedom I would need to look at my chains—those things that would prevent me from letting go. I would also need to avoid the spiritual blind alleys of blaming others for my problems, being too hard on myself, or getting discouraged. The desert fathers and mothers called me instead to be intrigued about where God was leading me in my life and where I was resisting it, and that was good.

What would help me with this? I would need to give myself a break in seeking what the *abbas* and *ammas* sought so I didn't discourage myself since this was a lifelong journey. In that vein, I would need to pace myself by appreciating that anything discovered doesn't need to be improved or even changed right on the spot. In looking at my life, I should not be negative or condemn anything but simply observe what I have learned— judgment would only waste energy and lead to some kind of criticism or defense. I simply needed to be practical enough to write down in my journal faithfully what I had observed.

The psychiatrist in me also would be helpful because I would be able to see where I was fighting self-awareness and becoming emotional because I had stopped simply observing and was now judging either myself or others. I also knew that, like anyone else, I would be tempted to avoid the real issues. Instead of doing this, I wanted to be more open, so I brought this up to Kathleen when I had the next opportunity, and she was very direct in her answer, which reminded me of how much I loved her sense of simplicity.

She said, "When you begin to get more and more excited about being open to spiritual wisdom and living a life filled with enjoying the gifts you have been given to share with others, the grace you receive will bear the following fruits :

Really being open to new learning—whether initially it is off-putting or seems positive

Enjoying picking up what your emotions are teaching you rather than defending yourself for feeling a particular way

Seeing the dangers of having too strong a preference for something rather than simply being receptive to it as a good when it is in your life

Allowing things you see to rest lightly

Appreciating the value of quiet meditation as a way to see all of these things

She then made a special point of returning me to the sayings of the desert because she said, "However, please remember what Abba Moses offered as simple advice for those disciples who approached him to seek what you are now seeking, namely, 'Go and sit in your cell and your cell will teach you everything.' What he was emphasizing is the central theme of the desert that 'constant prayer will quickly clear up your confusion.' It is important that you attend to what is important in order to live a life open to grace while not falling into the trap of making the spiritual journey into just another task that you do alone. God is with you and will lead you in the silence if you make space and listen. As you are doing right now, a little time in the morning to read Scripture and be quiet after it is a good start. Then during the day, taking a few breaths to reflect back on what the morning meditation offered you and a few moments in the evening to give the day back to God. Doing that is a good beginning."

"Is there anything else you can think of sharing with me?"

"Well, it is getting late, but let me leave you with a few 'words' as they did in the desert: *gratitude*—one of the *abbas* as he was dying said to those gathered around him for inspiration that to be saved they should: 'Rejoice always. Pray constantly. And, no matter what the circumstances, *give thanks.*'

"*Simplicity*—once again, we read from the sayings of the desert that we should not seek to fight all of our defeating, negative thoughts or temptations at the same time but instead find a central one and seek to speak to it with God at your side.

"And finally for now, let me reemphasize *Scripture* by closing with the words of the revered desert elder Abba Poemen who once said, 'The nature of water is yielding; whereas, the character of stone is that it is hard. Still, if you suspend a bottle filled with water above a stone so that the water can drip, drop by drop on the stone, eventually it will wear a hole in the stone. In a similar way, the Word of God is so tender, and we are hardhearted. Yet, when people are able to frequently hear the Word of God, their hearts can be opened, and they shall have a sense of awe with respect to God and they will be changed.'

"In light of what I have just said, the *ammas* and *abbas* of the desert did something quite simple that you do not yet do," she said to me. "Through reciting Scripture out loud when by themselves they began to learn Scripture *by heart* not just by memory. This will give you a well of healing water in having

these words at hand. And so, when you are sitting quietly—
especially when you are disturbed—start this desert approach
by going through the chapters of John's Gospel and such themes
and words of Jesus like the following ones will come to mind
from each of the Gospel's chapters:

Jesus is the light of the world
The call of Cana
People prefer the darkness
Living water offered to the Samaritan woman
Do you want to be made whole?
Food that does not perish
Thirst that will be quenched
Judgment
Seeing and Listening
I've come to bring you fullness
The resurrection theme of Lazarus's rising
Unless the wheat dies
Service as Jesus washes the feet of the disciples
Jesus's words, "I won't leave you orphaned, I will come
back for you."
"I've come to bring you fullness."
"Unless I leave the Paraclete cannot come."
"Don't take them out of the world but protect them."
"My kingdom is not of this world."
Jesus words from the cross: "Woman behold thy son;
son behold thy mother."

"My peace I leave to you."

"Come have breakfast.... Feed my sheep.... Follow me."

"Your words or theme taken from each chapter may be different than the ones I have just shared, but if you have them readily available to draw upon, you will have a reservoir of love and wisdom to join you in your silence alone, while driving, at a meeting, when emotional, *always and everywhere*."

With that, she became silent. Obviously, I had more than enough to reflect upon until our next, and as it turned out, quite fateful meeting.

A Good-Bye...for Now

For a number of weeks, I didn't sense Kathleen's presence. Finally, when I was by myself one evening, I couldn't take the silence and not knowing what was going on for another minute, so I spoke out in a voice a little stronger than I usually used with her, "I haven't seen you for a while, Kathleen. Is it because I am doing something wrong?"

Immediately, she responded in a gentle voice, "No, it is because you have done a lot that is right."

"So, all this silence isn't an indication that you are leaving me?" I asked.

"I will never leave you." If an angel can have emotion, I heard it in her words, and I filled up as well.

"So, what now?"

"You will continue to be who you are: wonderful, yet stumbling and doing silly things sometimes. I will be around but spending a bit more time on others who need more of my help."

"Okay. I think I understand." Then, as I sat there, something came to mind that I had asked about a long time ago, right after the deaths of my sister, Sheila, and the twins. "I still have two final questions which you never answered. Why is your name Kathleen, and why was it you that was sent to me?"

I could hear her laugh before she said, "Well, some people are scattered, and it is good to send a Guardian Angel named Greta to help them become a bit more organized. Others are very passionate, and they need a Placido to help calm them. You seemed to require both a light touch and a no-nonsense approach. They felt you also needed an Irish spirit with a twinkle in her eye and a bit of inherited wisdom to back her up, so they picked a 'Kathleen.'"

"Makes sense now that you put it that way. But I feel sad somehow even though you said some nice things about me just now. On the other hand, I sense that I should be happy that I've learned some important things from you and,"—I had a hard time uttering the last two words—"let go."

"Graduation from one stage to another is always both wonderful and a bit sad. No one wants to leave what they have finally mastered and the friends they have made. Yet, life changes, it always changes, and as you have helped your nieces and brother-in-law, Bill, learn, you have to let go."

"So, it is good-bye?"

"No. It is good-bye *for now*. I'll be around for a chat now and then and eventually will see you again."

"See?"

"Life goes quickly. Make the most of the beautiful days ahead by leaning back, enjoying the gifts of being alive, and sharing with others what you can."

"I will."

" I *know* you will." And then there was silence. Complete silence.

What I Learned about a Guardian Angel

There are more entries that I have in my journal, but I have shared enough with you for now. I hope that in some way my conversations with Kathleen will encourage you and those you love to enjoy your life more fully and share it more generously without expecting anything in return. If they don't, then I guess it was all in my head. On the other hand, if these interactions do actually prove helpful to you in the future, then I will know they were real and truly happened…at least in my heart.

As a psychiatrist, I have had many supervisors, teachers, and mentors through the years. However, when I think of Kathleen, I am reminded of what Carl Jung, one of the foremost psychiatrists of all time, used to ask, namely (and I am paraphrasing because I forget his exact words), "Where are the great, wise, and wonderful persons of old who did not merely talk about the meaning of life and the world but really possessed it?"

Kathleen was a sage like that. Because of her holiness, wisdom, and other charismatic gifts, she was able to help me uncover and face my fears, doubts, and distress, especially after the deaths of Sheila, Tom, and Jim. She was, as someone once said of the *ammas* and *abbas* of old, a "bearer of the Spirit" for me. I knew almost from the beginning that our relationship would lead me in different ways to flourish more richly and share more fully in a way that would also be natural and life-giving to others. However, what I admit to you and believe more firmly than ever is that I needed to commit myself to not simply admire her but also to take steps to emulate her. It was obvious to me that as an angel she didn't want me as a disciple for herself. Instead, through her guidance, she was setting the stage for me to stand on her wisdom so I could be in a better position to seek God directly for myself: a true desert journey.

What helped me make the most of my time with her, I think, was also that she was so non-defensive and open. Her attitude and deep abiding love for God were contagious as well. When I spent time with her, I not only felt better about myself and the joys of life but also really wanted to share all of this with others as I have finally begun to do now in letting you read this material from my journal.

When I think back about my time with Kathleen, I realize she even inspired me to look at those types of things that normally I would back away from. In my great desire to be free, open, and really mindful of each day, slowly I actually became intrigued even about such larger issues as where the meaning was in my life. I also became truly interested in any attachments or un-dealt-with anger that I had as well as such important discernments as where I was confusing comfortability with peace or satisfaction with deep inner joy. Without being judgmental in ways that would cause me to be defensive or self-indicting, I was even becoming fascinated with how I might be intolerant or resistant to intimacy with those who were different than I was and where I was being dishonest and protective even in my prayer life.

When I think of the times I spent with Kathleen, I feel as if I were sitting on a log in a forest in the Garden of Eden. With Kathleen there was little interest in the world as I know it, with its emphasis on money, image, power, glory, or position in life. Instead of playing the secular games of competition or seeking security or pleasure, I am now freer due to her help to explore the joy of living and sharing as I believe God originally meant it to be for us.

I'd like to think she sensed that appreciation in me because as a parting gesture she suggested that I read a story on un-self-conscious giving; she said that she thought as a psychiatrist I would especially enjoy it. It was from the writings of Taoist philosopher Chuang Tzu. While I thought finding it would really be impossible, after looking him up, I found that Thomas Merton had written a little paperback on him, *The Way of Chuang Tzu*, and the story was easy to find by paging through the brief book he had edited and for which he wrote a masterful introduction. It was marked by simplicity, as Kathleen was, and reading it once I had found the passage was a good way of concluding this phase of my conversations with my Guardian Angel, so I now offer it to you.

In an age when life on earth was full, no one paid any special attention to worthy men, nor did they single out the man of ability. Rulers were simply the highest branches on the tree, and the people were like deer in the woods. They were honest and righteous without realizing they were "doing their duty." They loved each other and did not know that this was "love of neighbor." They deceived no one yet they did not know that they were "men to be trusted."

They were reliable and did not know that this was "good faith."

They lived freely together giving and taking, and did not know that they were generous.

For this reason their deeds have not been narrated. They made no history.

When it became silent after her parting words, I thought: All that it would take now for me was to practice what Kathleen had taught me. Practice, practice, practice. Would I do it? Time certainly would tell. After being with Kathleen, what gave me a special sense of encouragement that I would follow through, though, was that I didn't need to succeed all the time in my efforts. I didn't need to stand out as being especially "religious" or "holy." My actions didn't need to make spiritual history.

I only needed to try to be as faithful as I could. Recognize when I wasn't. Ask God for forgiveness. Seek to do better. And move on. That was enough. That was more than enough…and, I believe, the same will be true for you.

ABOUT THE AUTHOR

Robert J. Wicks received his doctorate in psychology from Hahnemann Medical College and Hospital and is on the faculty of Loyola University, Maryland. He has published more than 50 books for professionals and the general public, including *Bounce: Living the Resilient Life; Riding the Dragon;* and *Perspective: The Calm Within the Storm.* He has received the Humanitarian of the Year Award from the American Counseling Association's Division on Spirituality, Ethics, and Values and in 2006 was recipient of the first annual Alumni Award for Excellence in Professional Psychology from Widener University.